Five Ordinary Men

Laurie Brady

Five Ordinary Men

Five Ordinary Men
ISBN 978 1 76109 655 6
Copyright © text Laurie Brady 2023
Cover image: Suzy at Pixabay

First published 2023 by
Ginninderra Press
PO Box 3461 Port Adelaide 5015
www.ginninderrapress.com.au

Contents

Terry Dunn

A manuscript retrieved by Simon Black
December 2022

Canst thou not minister to a mind

Diseased

Pluck from the memory a rooted sorrow,

Raze out the written troubles of the brain,

And with some sweet oblivious antidote

Cleanse the stuff'd bosom of that perilous stuff

Which weighs upon the heart?

W. Shakespeare, *Macbeth*. Act V, sc. iii

1

You won't believe me when I say I don't know why I did it. You'll think that sounds like an excuse. A reason in itself that may not explain but provides some sort of justification.

You won't ponder what I said, as if there could be something to it, something of substance that deserves consideration. Perhaps some things don't. You'll be outraged. I can hear it now. 'Who the hell does he think he is? Does he think we're complete idiots?'

Just stop and think about it, I should say to them. Can you really say, looking back on your life, that there has always been a reason for everything you've done? Wait a minute, I know your answer, so let me go on. That's only fair. There might be a reason if we accept the belief that there is an explanation for everything, every feeling, every action. There probably is. But how many of those reasons are known to us. Surely that's the crux of the matter.

Is it all so simple that we can say 'I did that because…'? Are we all so rational that we can say a certain feeling or emotion, a set of circumstances or something that's done to us, may lead us to engage in a particular action.

We're becoming philosophical now. Humans are different from animals, you'll say, because they have the power of reason. They can predict. They can hypothesise. They can see the consequences of their actions. And, yes, they are sufficiently advanced in their thinking to be able to explain, sometimes with help admittedly, why they behaved in a particular way.

'With help,' I just said. That brings something else into play. What help? A psychologist or is it a psychiatrist? You can't tell me that after hours on a couch pouring out my history of infant toilet habits, the pathos of unmet needs, oedipal leanings and adolescent rejections, if there were any, this stranger will be able to articulate, with the smallest grain of truth, why I did it.

Why shouldn't 'I don't know' be a sufficient reason? It's common enough. 'I don't know why that happened.' 'I don't know why she acted that way.' 'I don't know what I think about that.' Is it such a big leap to 'I don't know why I did it'?

You scoff of course. Hardly the same thing, you say. 'It's a bit different not knowing why something happened outside yourself', you say contemptuously, 'to knowing why you yourself acted in a particular way.' You might even concede there is a mix of reasons, but would go on to say that they can always be teased apart, like undoing a knot.

There was a boy at the school I went to. Brett Mullins. Nice boy. Reasonably intelligent. OK-looking. Came from a good family as far as it's possible to know. So no mileage there for you doubters. Anyway, one day after school he attacked this girl. Sidled up to her and hit her, and not just once. I can still remember her name. Fiona Berry. Quiet girl. Nice. Wouldn't hurt a fly. But she was hurt. Badly. Broken cheek bone, if I remember. Bung eye. Mullins didn't try to hide it. Several of us saw it. And when he was hauled into the principal's office, and later to the police, he didn't deny it. Said he didn't know why he did it. He even seemed baffled by it. Didn't even seem all that remorseful.

And before you wade in with your chorus of explanations, Fiona said she'd never argued with Mullins, they'd never really spoken to each other, and he hadn't made any advances that she'd rejected. Mullins said he'd always quite liked Fiona but had never had any strong feelings for her, which pours cold water on the idea of rampant adolescent hormones. He kept maintaining that he didn't know why he did it.

I later spoke to Mullins when it had all blown over and he'd paid harshly for it. Asked him if it had been another girl at the time, in the same place, and not Fiona, would he have done the same thing.

'Probably,' he said. Then he thought a little more, and said, 'I'm not sure.'

I regret not asking him what he might have done if it were a boy and not Fiona.

If I could see you now, I'd be watching the light dawning. A smirk, and 'Now we understand. Classic,' you'd say. 'Would have to be a sociopath or some other deviant.' I know the definitions. Someone with no empathy, no clear understanding of right and wrong.

You've got me there, but I don't think you're right. I know there are people like that, but they're few and far between, people who aren't normal, people who are seriously sick and need to be kept away from others in an institution. People who aren't sane. In one way, it proves my point that it's not always possible to know why we do something. But I wouldn't like you to think I'm one of them, or that what I said was based only on the mentally damaged. You know I'm not one of them. That's something else.

*

Let me tell you about Irene. Irene Susan Berridge. Of course, I only found out all this information some time later. Not that knowing these things would have changed anything.

Irene was born in Perth, and her parents moved to Sydney when she was finishing primary school. She attended Marden High, a co-educational state school in the north-west of Sydney, and from all reports was a good if not outstanding student. She was typical of the culture of the time, a reasonably affluent period in our history, upwardly mobile middle-class ethos nourished by church-belt values. Hard-working, thrifty, ethical, respectful.

Irene was petite, pretty and animated, the sort of spiritedness or vibrancy that needed to be lit by another, coaxed out from a natural reticence. Sandy shoulder-length hair and slightly protuberant blue eyes that seemed to express wonder.

'She was quite something' in those days, a former boyfriend told me. Photographs confirmed it. 'Lovely figure.' One that naturally thickened with approaching middle-age.

She studied Arts at Sydney University, a suite of subjects pejoratively called 'Matrimony One' because it didn't seem to have a finite career end. The prediction was realised soon after when she married an unlikely partner of mixed ethnic origin, a marriage that lingered painfully for three years before an acrimonious divorce.

A period of exaggerated sexual activity followed the breakdown. Not unusual. A hitting out. It's difficult to say whether it was the telltale reaction to disillusionment with her ex-partner, or a response to the middle-class constraints and sanctimony of her adolescent years. Probably both.

She was left depressed and unhappy, and was often given to fits of crying. Her many friends were supportive. She relied heavily on the doting support of her younger brother, and her ageing uncomprehending parents.

But new growth insensibly buds, and Irene settled down, or settled for a more even life. She trained as a teacher of languages, finding new purpose and acceptance in teaching. She continued to date, though more selectively, and from all reports showed a reluctance to commit. Once-bitten? Who knows?

She lived alone in a townhouse in North Parramatta which she took great pride in decorating. The years settle. They also have a way of putting a brake on the desire to change. So they did with Irene.

How do I know all this? I made it my business to find out. Don't ask me how. No one is an island.

You may wonder why I'm giving an account, however brief, of Irene's life. She barely has a word in the plot. She's only a very minor character, but she is also pivotal. That will become apparent later. She was thirty-five when we met. Our one brief meeting.

*

I need to tell you about Lake Parramatta. Not that I think context, this context, perhaps any context, has a great deal of relevance.

Parramatta is a thriving city to the north of Sydney that was booming in those years as western Sydney was being developed with a vengeance. The lake is a recreation park to the south of the city. The large lake fans out from a number of feeding rivers, and is contained at one point by an impressive dam. There's a patrolled swimming area, canoes and paddle boats for enthusiasts, a children's playground, a small café that caters for morning teas and lunches, and expansive grassy areas. It is beautifully maintained and very picturesque. Tall gums claw their way into rock that edges the lake. Wattle yellows the foreshore in season, and there's enough birdlife to satisfy the enthusiast.

People come for a picnic, or to take the rocky but easy-going track that winds through scrubland and rainforest for four kilometres around the perimeter of the lake. I've taken the walk several times, sometimes alone, and sometimes with a friend. It's a pleasant experience because you always meet walkers coming from the other direction, and stop to chat, often meeting afterwards to renew contact in the café.

The day in question was a warm autumn day, but it was overcast. A cobalt sky smeared with a deep rinse of purple. There'd been a light shower an hour earlier, only enough to tickle my bare arms, a foreshadowing of what might come. I debated whether I should set out. The walk would take a little over an hour, and if it rained, there was no protection.

I stalled for time, waiting in the café, having my customary hot mocha. I never had to order. They knew me there, or at least knew my face, and the girl who made the coffee always made a design on the surface of it. We'd laugh about it, with me calling for something more ornate each time, and so the designs became more elaborate.

'Communing with nature'. I don't like that expression. Such a cliché. Is it because it suggests some religious or semi-mystical experience? Perhaps that's fair enough. If God is anywhere, he must be here. I enjoy the orchestra of the bush, the coloured reflections in the mirror of the lake, and the sweeping blue canvas of sky. It's also where I come for inspiration. I sometimes like to write, and it's a fertile place for ideas.

*

I decided to risk it. How often do we deny ourselves to find there was no need to do so? The sky had lightened to a sweat of mauve. It wasn't raining. The serving girl in the café wished me luck, shaking her head at my foolishness and smiling.

The walk begins with steps that lead down to skirt the lake before the track opens and climbs to a rock platform and a panorama in all directions. I stopped to look. I always do. To the south, the sky was a benign grey; to the north, a threatening charcoal. I decided to press on, even though the bush orchestra had taken its instruments and gone home. It must have been a warning.

After several hundred metres, the track narrows and falls steeply to a creek, crossing to rise on the other side. This is the southern point of the ellipse. Too late to turn back now. The track emerges on a long disused gravel road before it re-enters the bush after a short distance.

I was enjoying myself. After all this time, I can still remember what I was thinking as I walked. I'd given a presentation at work that had been a great success. Interesting, isn't it, how we sometimes position a circumstance by an altogether different memory, one that remains with us.

The rain came without warning, a surprise. The dark clouds were further to the north. All I could do was run for the nearest tree that might give some protection. It was only metres from the water that was roughed up and dimpled with rain. There was no way to avoid getting wet.

She came from the opposite direction, and seeing me dripping beneath a gum with a sparing canopy, hurried across to join me. She was better prepared for the weather than me. Decked out in military green wet weather gear and hood. We laughed. I made some joke about the beautiful autumn weather. She answered saying she'd get out the picnic things from her small rucksack. We laughed again and were silent.

That's when I struck. She fell heavily, and was motionless for a few seconds. Her rucksack had come off in her fall, the hood fell from her head, and she rolled the few metres to the lake in slow motion as if she was being drawn towards it.

Some of you might want detail. I can't give it. I don't remember a splash as she rolled into the lake. One moment she was there. Then she wasn't. I don't remember seeing her face or hearing a cry. It was all so still. Eerily quiet. Forgive the cliché, but time had stopped. I do remember stepping to the edge, and seeing her body that had landed on a ledge in a metre of brown pocked water before it disappeared into the deep.

Why? Why, you ask. And I can't answer. She didn't say anything to provoke me. Didn't do anything. She was pleasant. I liked her. Even now I think of Brett Mullins all those years ago looking baffled. There must have been a reason, but it was hidden like Irene was in the muddy depths.

So what did I feel? It should have been shock and horror. It wasn't. I should have rushed to rescue her as she rolled towards the water, tried to revive her, apologised, if it wasn't already too late. I didn't. But I'm avoiding what you want to know. My feeling. If anything, it was a mild curiosity, more of a nullity.

It was still raining when I threw her rucksack into the lake. It floated for several seconds before it was overwhelmed by the water and disappeared. I didn't complete the walk but returned the way I'd come, wet through. The Muslim girl who made the coffee in the café waved, grinning. I should have known better. I got into my car and drove home.

*

Irene Susan Berridge. What's in a name? Meaning, of course. Words, names give a thought, a feeling and an action, a reality. I didn't want to know. It seemed to colour what I'd done. Gave my action a meaning it didn't have before. It would have been better if she'd remained anonymous. I could have avoided the newspapers and their reports of a missing person. But something made me want to know, not to savour it, that's the last thing I'd have wanted, but to explain it to myself.

I expected to be interviewed but I wasn't. Irene had walked the kilometre from her townhouse to the lake, so there was no parked car to tell where she might be. She hadn't told anyone where she was going, and she was planning to visit the café for her coffee when she'd finished the walk. Not before. So she hadn't been seen. A police woman later asked at the café but they couldn't help.

It remains a mystery to this day. There was no secret love affair or jilted lover that might explain foul play. She wasn't depressed. There was certainly no dementia that might have explained her wandering away.

It was some time before I visited the lake again, but I always stop my walk at the creek crossing.

2

My name's Terry Dunn. Christened Terence James Dunn. I'm forty as I write this. Isn't that what they used to call the beginning of middle age? I think those labels have changed by a decade now. Fifty's the new forty, and so on.

Memory sometimes creeps up and surprises us, slipping through our defences. But I want to tell you about myself so that you might better understand what must have shocked you. I'll try to pluck some of the memories like picking pilling off a woollen pullover.

When I was one, my family moved to Epping from Homebush and into a modest two-bedroom apricot-brick house. It was my parent's first real home as they'd been living with my father's sister. I can only imagine my father's pleasure struggling to reveal itself on a face that was a study of restraint, a face that baulked at showing excitement and that analysed the world through remarkably blue eyes.

He was strict. Parents of that generation were. But he was fair. If my brother and I wanted anything, even reassurance or affection, we were to go to him. His image of indulgent fatherhood was being approached by his sons for help or advice. Not his coming to us. King in his sacred realm. This lack of immediacy frustrated me as I grew older.

Average height, mid-brown hair with balding crown, he'd leave for work in his homburg hat in the old Ford Prefect. Why am I a little saddened by that image, one that does creep up? It was typical of the times. Life was so simple.

He was a good man. How often do you hear that? A common judgement of fathers by this generation of knowing children. 'He was a good man.' I always think it sounds too bald, as if it leaves something unsaid.

My mother was probably typical of the times. A homemaker. Gentle, yielding, practical. She was always putting my brother and me first. Of course, when you're a child, you never consider that. Wasn't it what all mothers did? Only years later did I question such unselfishness. Might it mean that you saw yourself as less worthy than others?

Short, pretty with jet-black hair, and always on the go, she happily accepted without question what the world offered or imposed. I can't remember seeing her deep in thought, or hearing her discussing a social or political issue as I so often did with my father. A moderately self-made man, having left school at the intermediate certificate, my father's small library included Kant, Descartes, Emerson, Shaw and Wilde. My mother was content with a good novel.

Recalling all this has brought to mind an incident that captures one difference between them. I was finishing sixth class at school, the last year before high school. The two major prizes at the end of year speech night were Dux of the School and Citizen of the Year. I was no hope for the first, but I'd been very active helping others in the school and community. Always wanting to impress. I don't think I had my mother's altruism.

It may not seem much to me now, but looking back it was huge. I was overwhelmed when my name was read out. Walking on air to the stage, climbing the steps, receiving an inscribed trophy from some important politician, the clapping and later the slaps on the back from well-meaning friends.

My mother and father were proud. It was stamped on their faces. Once we'd returned home, they were both generous with their praise. My mother came to me, and hesitated for a second, before she reached out and hugged me. It was brief, a second or two before she withdrew, but it was a hug. I think my father began to open his arms as he walked the few paces towards me. I can't be sure. It may have been his gait. I do remember a few awkward seconds as he stood there, before he reached out to shake my hand.

Paul. I haven't mentioned Paul, my brother. Two years older. Chalk and cheese. Isn't that what people say about the difference between siblings? It seems to be more common in families than not.

I might have been shy, but I was outgoing. Paul was more reserved. Perhaps not willing to risk emotion's trade. Our parents knew. It was apparent in the pullovers my mother lovingly knitted for us. Red or yellow for me. Blue or green for Paul. More about him later.

I have few memories of my infant years. Some people remember details. I don't. Those first years were an endless blur of nights and days. There was no bigger scheme for calibrating life. But my boyhood is rich in memories.

One image that always returns of our family togetherness is our Sunday outings in the Ford Prefect. My seat was behind the driver, my father. My mother didn't drive. I'd peer from the window, steaming it with my breath to finger it with my initials, T.D. I'd watch the open fields hurtle by, scrub and straw-coloured grass beneath an endless sky. I'd watch my father's long-lobed ears and the silver hairs that sprouted on his neck, and feel a strange tenderness I didn't understand. I know now it was an awareness of our fallibility, something we all share.

My mother encouraged us to sing with her in the car. It was her idea of family harmony. Along with dinner table conversation and playing charades. A happy family sing together. I knew it was important for her and joined in. Paul didn't.

These softer feelings disappeared when I left the car to squabble with Paul and dispute the injustice of adult law.

On weekends, I'd play with Johnny Reid in our cubby house, an old wooden packing case for a car that my father set up against a side fence between privets. The window he cut at the end helped us to imagine it as a plane, ship, submarine and rocket, even if it did look out on waste building material and garden rubbish. We conquering heroes always returned from our adventures in time for mother's morning tea caramel slice.

For a half day each weekend, I had to help in the garden. We lived on a large tapering block of land that my father decorated with dozens of stone-edged gardens. This of course meant that half of them were always choked with weeds. It was impossible to reach the end. I can see him now on his haunches, thrashing clods of earth against the spade to free the soil with its fat worms from the weeds.

I wondered why he didn't settle for having fewer gardens, planting large shrubs and keeping more lawn. But he had a vision. Don't we all? I believe my expected help was a strategy to teach me responsibility. And an opportunity for communion – there, I've said it again – with his sons.

I often fought with Paul. We were both competitive. Thinking about what's happened since, I regret some of the things I said to him, but they were probably no worse than normal sibling hostility. It wasn't all bad. We shared a bedroom in our boyhood years, and would lie in bed, verbally improvising our own serials until we fell asleep.

With what I told you happened at Lake Parramatta, you might be expecting an account of a bleak childhood. It wasn't. There were many happy times. I've mentioned some of them. And of course birthdays with class friends invited. And Christmas. Christmas dinners with the extended family, exchanging gifts, and puddings with threepences and brandy sauce.

I have a Christmas photograph of a family 'gallery of rogues', an aunt, vanilla-scented, releasing anxiety with intermittent laugh, another aunt, nonchalant and thinking of more exciting times, her husband, bland and unsmiling behind thick-lensed glasses, and my mother with her nursing eyes.

For the young Terry Dunn, home was a place you learned to eat and sleep, and love. Did I say love? When I was ten, I received a note from nine-year-old Susie Walker a few doors away. It read, 'If you love me like I love you, only death can part us two.' I'd have been delighted to receive that note from Susie five years later, but at the time I didn't know how to reply, probably didn't feel the same, and did nothing. My father spoke gently to me a week later about how I should have behaved, to avoid hurting Susie. She had been upset that I hadn't replied, and our fathers had talked about it.

*

My primary school years were not unhappy. Wait a second. I said 'not unhappy'. I didn't say 'happy'. There might be a shade of difference there.

My teachers were kind, but there were a few in the school who weren't. I was a good student. Average intelligence, but eager to please. I did what I was told. No trouble.

They were the days before caning disappeared. Next door to my third-class room, there was a single class of older boys doing a strand of technical education. One day, one of the older boys came to our door asking if Mr Niland from next door could borrow the cane. Half a minute later, there was a mighty crack like a rifle shot, shortly followed by another, and the same boy returned red-faced to return the cane.

I've never forgotten it. I was horrified, and for years after I imagined with a morbid fascination what it must have looked like next door. Like an execution. At the time, I was left wondering why my classmates didn't feel the same.

I played the obligatory games of marbles, collected cigarette cards and Matchbox toys, and in sixth class swapped conversation lollies with a girl I liked. Conversation lollies were flat sweets the size of a fifty-cent coin that had messages printed on them. The mere fact of a message, any message, was what made them prized, even if, like 'Sweet Sixteen', the message had no literal relevance for eleven-year-olds.

Co-education hadn't bloomed yet, and while we were all in the same school, the sexes were housed in different buildings, and had to play in different playgrounds. It was forbidden to mingle.

I was once caught talking to a girl, and racing her up and down the yellow line that divided the two playgrounds. Strange, but I still re-member her name. Jennifer Dibley.

Mr Wood asked me if what he'd been hearing was true. 'No, sir,' I said without even asking what he'd heard. How was I to know it was a test, that he'd been watching from the window?

'You have to take responsibility for your actions, Terry,' he said. 'You will always have responsibilities, and for every action there is a conse-quence.' And the consequence was painful.

In my final year, our class met with a class of fifth-class girls for folk dancing. It must have been a syllabus directive to allow some interaction of the sexes before we were all consigned to heterosexual hell. The first of the two classes to arrive would stand around the inner of two concentric circles. The students in the second class to arrive would stand behind a partner. Teachers would sometimes turn a blind eye to students who stood behind a favoured partner rather than move around the circle in line.

I was one who had a favoured partner. Two actually. Narelle and Sylvia. They were soft and compelling. Bewitching. They even smelled different. The static from the amplifiers on the building wall was the first music for my budding romanticism, loping around the circle with something like the Canadian three step.

Talking of music, I was in the school band. Flutes and drums. I was a flautist. Our role was to march the children into their classrooms, and to play at community functions. For them, we'd dress in our navy woollen shorts and socks, white shirt with red tartan sash, and a navy brimless hat with crest that was something like you might see in an academic procession. How many times did I listen to the palaver of a community dignitary offering specious optimism for the future when there were boys like us as models?

I studied at home in a downstairs tool room that I shared with Paul. I worked at a large trestle table that was painted in a bright yellow gloss. Rough wooden boxes labelled with the peeling paper stickers of Perry's Fruit and Veg were used to store my workbooks. The light was dim, and criss-crossing pipes often whined with the house's plumbing. There was a trapdoor beside my desk, opening into the underneath bowels of the house, and from it there were often scurrying noises, probably possums. As the older, Paul had a desk and more congenial working conditions.

I'd better stop. Recall like this is self-perpetuating. One memory ignites another. I could go on forever. For those of you seeking an explanation for what I did some time ago, I don't suppose this was much help. But people can do with data what they will, and come up with surprising explanations.

There's always the danger too in thinking back that memories may be fictions that have been made real when thinking makes them so. I've often wondered if memories change as we grow, reworked by the insights that time provides to fit the meanings we now want to believe. It's up to you to decide.

3

You might be thinking the story's moved on, that what happened at Lake Parramatta is all but forgotten, lost in the muddy waters of time, the amnesia of history. That isn't true.

Part of me wants to understand why, particularly when the story of the lake is far from over. But the other part tells me there's no knowing, that life can never be that simple. Must there be an answer to everything? Am I rambling on with this account believing that one of you will suddenly shout Eureka, and everything will be explained? No. I wish there was such an explanation. Perhaps then I could be typed, noteworthy like the butterfly pinned to a corkboard in the museum with a Latin tag, and a detailing of its strange doings.

I will continue. If there is to be an explanation, I'm the only one to provide it. Besides, telling you all this is catharsis for me.

*

When I was fourteen, I moved into the small sunroom next to the kitchen. My parents thought it was time I had my own room. It was small, but big enough for a bed, a desk, and a single standing cupboard for clothes. It looked over the garden to a million city lights, and at night I could see a feast of stars piercing the sky with my longings.

I could hear the television in the lounge room with its canned hysterics mocking my studies and bedside prayer. Everything outside was heavy with meaning. Insights emerged and were nursed. My changing emotions cooked in a stew of imaginings. The pittosporum tapped the window near my bed with its nutty fingers. My room was the cave to which I was glad to return.

At six p.m., I was often awakened to my mother in the kitchen beyond my door lighting the gas stove and making the porridge. I didn't think much about it then, but it later became a symbol in those uncertain teenage years, a symbol of security like the dogged love that was palpable if not openly shown.

I know what you're thinking. Oedipus. Mother love. I'm sure you're wrong, but Freud would say such feelings are unconscious. So who's to know? I will admit to a slight antipathy towards my father, a protest that he could have done more to help my mother.

One day I opened a drawer to find my father's service medals among bric-a-brac, bulldog clips, used batteries, nail clippers, erasers, and was reminded of his wartime travels in the middle east, and the furry copies of his travels he'd written, typed on my mother's Remington. I was ashamed then. He was a victim as we all were of time and culture's pitiless conspiracy.

A year later, I started to attend 'fellowship'. That's what we all called it. A youth group affiliated with the local church. Hour-long meetings with prayer, singing and a guest speaker would take place an hour before the evening church service so we could attend both. We'd also visit other Christian groups with a fine octet, and one of us would give the address. Several times a year, there was a fellowship tea attended by up to two hundred. We all contributed.

The tone of both the fellowship and church was didactic but too uncertain of itself to be sanctimonious. There were no formal prohibitions, but you don't need constraints to be made official before they're felt.

We didn't understand that then. Like my mother, we accepted the culture that owned us. It was a wall built around us. But aren't we all building our own walls to protect ourselves from threat, real or imagined? Most of us never see the walls that rise invisibly. Those who do, and try to knock them down, often find that they have already crumbled.

I wasn't aware of a wall. It was the way things were. Fellowship and church gave the Christian message. It gave answers. Answers that could be accepted or tweaked. It also provided contact with like-minded boys of the same age. And girls.

I had a few girlfriends in the fellowship, though I laugh when I think of how 'girlfriend' is interpreted now. Genital greetings. With Trish, two years younger from a born-again family, and Faye, intelligent and driven, I may have held hands or even stolen a kiss. No more. Relationships evolved. No one was sure how. They were something you fell into. Usually short-lived, not able to penetrate deep enough to go further.

Religion is often blamed for mental illness, just as it is for social unrest. But Christian dogma and its ally guilt were not part of my reckoning. At least, I wasn't aware that they were.

Years later, I'm still meeting friends from the fellowship days. I swap news with Simon about what's happened to some of them. We agree it was an important foundation for what we believe now. But was it a foundation to cling to, or one to depart from? Both, I think.

*

Simon. Simon Black. My best friend then and now. Simon is two years older. His more pronounced baldness is no indication of the difference in our ages. That can happen at any age, and for him is at odds with the youthful face that always looks upon the world with a contentment and kindness.

That's an odd thing I've just said. Faces on the whole don't reveal anything. What can you make of a nose, ear or chin, though lines in certain places may give a clue? It's all in the eyes. His are pale blue-grey, and they fix you with a warmth and don't let go.

Born in Queensland, his family moved to Epping when he was nine and sent him to a prestigious boys' private school. He excelled both in the classroom and on the sporting field, and trained to be a doctor at the University of New South Wales. Closeted for six years of medical training, his rare social outlet was the fellowship at St Albans. He came at the same time I did, and with the same innocence and naïveté.

He has an older sister who helps him in his medical practice, but he always makes time for our monthly meetings for coffee.

Kindness can be a cross to bear if it's partnered with a lack of discernment, and Simon paid the price. He's happily married now but only after a bitter first divorce and two girls who are jealously guarded by their unbalanced mother. But those things are beyond the scope of my story.

There's no defining moment in how our relationship grew. I can't remember, and Simon can't either. There was a girl Simon fancied in the fellowship. We still talk about her. Joanne Stead. My image has faded, washed out by the years. But I remember a tall willowy girl with green eyes, shoulder-length brown hair and a soft but deliberate way of speaking.

He must have confided his infatuation. Perhaps I asked. I think that was the beginning for us. Each week, we'd talk about it after fellowship or church. Had anything happened? Had he spoken to her? I can almost hear you laughing. Why didn't he just walk up and ask her out, you're saying.

I was the same. What you're suggesting was big then. For us, if not others. Remember what I said about falling into relationships. Imagine the gawky young hero of a music hall production trying to reveal his heart to the equally as innocent and bemused heroine, but failing from fear of being too forward. That was us. But Simon and Joanne didn't fall. Into a relationship, that is.

Time moved quickly from the fellowship days. The culture changed. We can laugh about it now, but those encounters, or want of encounters, were part of the stew of wild imaginings in my bedroom chrysalis at night.

Nothing happened with Joanne. We left the fellowship to pursue our different lives. We can't remember when Joanne left. For Simon, she remains a memory of what might have been.

*

I was mowing the lawn when Paul died. I was eighteen. The mower was razing the silver whiskers of frost and had stopped. The news came by phone. I was lucky to hear it ringing. My parents were not at home to receive it. They were on a trip to the Dubbo zoo with their lawn bowls club.

Paul's girlfriend Zina had been driving the car that ran off the road near Wollombi, threaded its way down an incline through trees and came to rest upside down in several metres of freezing water. Zina floated free. Paul didn't.

My reaction was one of disbelief. Sometimes, emotion lags behind a shock. It needs time to settle. Its impact did follow, more as an opiate of misery without real feeling, a numbness. Apart from the unexpected in relationships, it was the first real challenge to my life of certainties.

It was fortunate that my mother had left details of where they could be contacted. I phoned immediately, asking for my father, more fearful of how the news would affect my mother. I'll never forget that phone call, my father's palpable struggle, his need to critique, to control, the helplessness disguised as collaboration – 'So what do you think we should do, Terry?' – my mother's urging for news in the background, knowing something was wrong, his telling her, and the sounds of her hysteria and women flocking to comfort.

It was probably a typical coping with grief for that generation, my mother's pain without check, and my father's male stoicism and struggling faith in reason.

I'd later have nightmares of seeing Paul in the throes of death, the knotted cords bulging in a face pressed flat against the window of an upturned car, swaying with the current's pearl and lime-bright weeds.

I met my mother and father at Cessnock hospital, imagining Paul lying somewhere there in final wooden sleep, and thought of how, as a devotee of taste he would rate this end. I remember being unusually aware of the details of hospital lawn, the textured brick and struggling flowers, searching for meaning or symbols.

I went with my father to the mortuary annex, where my father viewed Paul's body. We thought it would upset my mother to do so. She agreed. My father emerged pale-faced, a hint of trembling about a clenched mouth. I don't know why I didn't go inside. If it's supposed to help us accept the awful finality, I didn't need to be convinced. If it's supposed to be an opportunity for a final goodbye, to who or what are we saying goodbye? Was I a coward?

When we entered the police station, the eyes of the pretty constable anticipated pettiness. 'The neighbours poisoned all our shrubs.' 'The cat's stuck in a pipe.' That changed. There was silence and concern as I explained. Eyes searched my face. Were they trying to glean some understanding of what had happened from blood likeness? My mother took the watch and sodden wallet with a moan.

For years, I'd escape to the veranda in dead of night and hug the cold. The sentience of the bush with its heavy scents and cricket noises would bring Paul near. We had never been close. Perhaps death unites.

I've kept a photograph of him. Framed it. It sits on my bedroom dresser gathering dust with those of my parents. It's the enigmatic Paul, but with his usual indifference warmed with an ironic smile. Does anyone wonder now whether he once felt a searing love, a rarefied emotion, whether he railed against injustice or retreated like a child? Does anyone care? Anyone?

*

'Why Arts Law?' Simon asked.

We were having our monthly morning tea meeting at a café in Epping. An attractive woman in her early thirties and wearing a tailored suit walked past.

'You haven't lost it yet,' Simon quipped. 'She couldn't take her eyes off you.' '

I'm quite sure she was looking at you,' I replied.

That was typical of our banter. We'd tease each other, flirt with the waitresses. But there was no self-delusion. It was part of our mythology.

Operating within the law gives everyone an agreed upon blueprint for how to behave, what society has decided is right and wrong. That's how I answered Simon.

'But is society always right?' he replied. 'Don't they, society that is, often get it wrong? I imagine all of us have done something at some time, however small, that society, or the law might frown upon.'

I agreed with him that the law was imperfect, and asked him if he thought there was a better way. Would he be happy to leave it up to individuals to decide what worked for them, whatever the consequences were for others? I knew he'd never accept that. It was a lame argument, and neither of us wanted to go on with it.

Simon was beginning his third year of Medicine. I still lived at home, and would catch the train from Epping to Redfern and walk to Sydney University. I found university an overwhelming change from school. Large lecture rooms housed hundreds of students. Tutors resorted to looking at the pages of a class list to ask some anonymous student a question, always prefaced by Mr or Miss. It was easy to be lost, to feel that the world had grown too big, and you were ever so small.

I'd always been a slave to time, and study demanded a routine. Time became more important, and I began to give myself small rewards when I'd been happy with the work I'd completed. Half an hour's television. The luxury of a phone call. Lying on the bed for fifteen minutes to indulge the recent fantasy.

We still went to fellowship. With the time-consuming demands of study, it had become an even more important outlet. Usually the only one. Many of us were university students, so work demands on all of us were comparable.

Serious relationships were rare. We'd sometimes find time in university holidays to go out in a mixed group. Once, we went to the lake. It might have been my idea. Simon was carrying on passionately about some issue, over balanced and fell in the water. Hysterical laughter was soon followed by concern. He had disappeared in deep water. I was overcome by a strange sensation. A fear. A sickening feeling. Others must have seen it.

But he soon appeared to our cheers, with strands of water weed draped over his head, and, always equal to the occasion, made a plaintive quack. It became folklore.

I had my first sexual experience in my first year at university. Xanthe Clark was four years older than me. Yes, the older woman. It was probably a fantasy in my night-time imaginings. Xanthe had travelled widely. Raised in England before moving here as an adult, she may have been of the world, having been to France, Spain, even the Solomon Islands, but she was not worldly, certainly not sophisticated. She was athletic-looking, with a figure most would call well-endowed. Tall, loose-limbed and hazel-eyed with a rosy English complexion, she greeted people with a winning naivety. She'd had one sexual partner, who I gathered from our talks had something to do with her lack of confidence.

She was not a fellowship girl. I'd sometimes travel with her on the train to and from university. She lived in Epping. I was surprised to be invited to a party in the unit she owned one Saturday night, and even more surprised when she asked me if I'd like to stay as others were leaving. I was in no hurry to get home.

As the last guest left, she made fresh coffee and we sat on the lounge sharing our experiences in a way we hadn't on the train. We spoke of the people and things that were important to us. We began to hold hands. I don't know who took the initiative. I wasn't aware of when it happened. It hardly matters.

Such talk can be an aphrodisiac when common ground is realised. We kissed, gently at first, then with greater feeling. We held each other awkwardly on the lounge, not able to get close enough, until she took my hand and stood. I'd just confided my naivety and inexperience with the opposite sex, so I imagine she felt comfortable taking the lead. There comes a point, doesn't there, when understanding is mutual, and when what follows is destined?

I know what you're going to say. 'We don't need to hear any more. Isn't it sufficient to simply say you had sex? To keep going on about it is gratuitous, even pornographic.'

I don't agree. If this exercise is one of soul-searching for me, and understanding for you, it's important that I share what happened, and what I was thinking, particularly as the incident was an intimate one, one that may have significance.

In her bedroom, we stood before the dressing mirror at the foot of the bed and undressed each other. Slowly. We weren't embarrassed. I was surprised by that. Surprised that I was no longer the bumbling music hall hero. What had happened to change me?

I remember her pleased smile, a flicker of pride as I admired her nakedness marbled by the moon lodged in a windowpane. And I remember her taking my hand and ever so gently leading me to the bed. I think that simple gesture of care, almost a reverence, meant as much to me as what followed.

When it was over, she curled up beside me with her head on my shoulder. I could feel the warmth of her thigh, the tickle of her hair. I lay on my back watching the moon play tricks on the ceiling, asking myself if this was as good as it gets, for how was I to know, and feeling a slight loss of control after the years of tortured self-denial.

We repeated the experience once and parted friends. Xanthe married shortly afterwards.

4

Sometimes, the greatest influence on abnormal, or even out of the ordinary behaviour, is the least obvious. It might be a whole mix of unmet needs, scorned proposals or subtle abuse. Not the more dramatic and obvious like an assault, a betrayal, a divorce or the bereavement of a love one.

You've all seen someone suddenly erupt with no apparent provocation. It may be an innocent word or phrase that is a trigger for the outburst, something that cuts deep. And you look on with disbelief in a hushed room as the embarrassed speaker keeps repeating, 'But what did I say, I only said…'

I think we've all been there. Hurt by something that was never intended to hurt. We usually know why when we've had time to think about it. But not always.

The incident with Irene at the lake is not far away in this potted history. I'm about to report a painful event in my life, but you shouldn't be too hasty in thinking that I've been teasing you to this point in the story, only now about to reveal a more plausible explanation. Surely it's all relevant.

*

Pam Baker was born in Sydney and reared in Rydalmere, a semi-commercial suburb in the north-west. Her parents were caring, her father self-employed, and her mother committed to looking after Pam, her two brothers and a younger sister. The family moved to Eastwood as Pam was finishing school, and she was increasingly needed to shoulder responsibilities in the home as her mother's medical condition deteriorated. Her sister and brothers were little help.

It was a tribute to her ability and determination that she was accepted to study Arts at Sydney University, and later to train as a high school teacher of modern languages. Given her mother's condition, the usual country service was waived, and Pam was appointed to Malvina High, a short drive from her Eastwood home.

I first met Pam at West Head, a lookout with spectacular coastal views in Kuring-gai Chase National Park. Attractive, brown-haired and green-eyed, there was something even then about Pam that gave the impression of being sound. What do I mean by that? Balanced. Even, I suppose. Feet firmly on the ground. This balance was reflected, probably nurtured by the challenges she faced at home, in the considered opinions she expressed to me, and to my often-dissenting father, always tempered by diplomacy.

'We can guess what's coming,' you're saying. 'You and Pam. How the relationship grew. The romance. Do we really need to know that? It can hardly be relevant, can it?'

Not entirely perhaps. I plead context again. It helps give a fuller picture of me. I think you can allow me a little latitude.

It was one of those rare times for both of us when we wanted to be alone, to get away from home and take stock. She was there when I arrived, sitting and looking over the low stone wall, across the silvered water to Palm Beach. We were the only two there, so it wasn't unusual for us to drift together. Casual talk morphed into more serious sharing.

Using each other as a sounding board for our thoughts was binding. Something was happening even then. *Frisson*. Perhaps that's too strong a word. It was certainly pleasant.

We took a rough track that fell to a beach, invisible from the lookout. The sun flared silver on the water, the sand was littered with pieces of driftwood, cones had fallen from the thick surrounding shrubs, and large lizards sunned themselves on massive boulders. Enough description. Our experiences are coloured by our emotions. We kissed. Enough said.

Approaching the beach as two, that was no longer the case as we made our way back to the lookout. I felt the awe of something growing, something I hadn't experienced before. Something pregnant with excitement. She later told me she felt the same.

There's no café at West Head, so we drove, with her following me, to Church Point, where we lunched at the Waterfront Café and General Store, later taking our shoes off, rolling up our trousers, and wading in the warm green shallows.

And so it began. They were happy months as we started to really know each other. Of course, every growing relationship has its moments. There are times when the magic disappears, and the man and woman find themselves back to the loneliness that first led them to finding each other. The experience has been so perfect that it can't be sustained, tensions emerge and become quarrels, even anger. But being apart can't be endured, and they are driven together again. It was no different for us. In that way, lover's quarrels became a renewal of love.

It was a time when couples didn't always talk openly. It was probably an age when we didn't have the insights that the modern generation has, an age when issues were left to gather weight.

Pam and I were proud that our disagreements were settled without too much fuss. There were no disputes over money, and sex had its allocated place.

We were married at St Jude's Anglican Church in Dural, an old nineteenth-century stone church. Simon was best man, and Pam's younger sister was bridesmaid. The reception followed at Araluen, an old stately home in Epping.

There were a couple of happy years, times when we giggled together like children, cried together, and lay in each other's arms feeling something of the awe we felt that first day at West Head.

So what went wrong? I don't want to give details. I can't. I get annoyed by those who expect some simple answer. Rarely is there only one. It might be true when there is domestic violence or cheating involved, but it's usually more complex than that. And the reasons a person gives for the breakdown often change over the months and years with each revisiting. Some details diminish in importance. Others assume greater significance. Until the revisiting stops, one explanation settles and is adopted as the most likely. Or all are rejected.

As things became worse between us, Pam insisted on counselling. We attended a few sessions but stopped when the counsellor, undertaking what I believed to be an impossible task of teasing out what was wrong, seemed to show more sympathy for me than her.

I believe now that her call for counselling was a subterfuge, a way of justifying her decision to an unforgiving world that she'd later court with tales of my shortcomings. The decision had already been made. The counselling was a charade, an acting out of a deluded self-righteousness.

Towards the end, she moved into the second bedroom and treated me with a restrained politeness. From outward appearances, things looked normal. We continued with the work around the house we usually did, though she was getting home later and later as the end neared.

She made the final decision one Saturday morning as I was preparing breakfast, asking me to sit at our kitchen bench, telling me she had something important to say. Of course, I knew what was coming. I suppose there's a point in doomed relationships when something formidable that has been lost can never be reclaimed.

She wanted me to go, to leave her with the house, at least for now, to settle what needed to be done later. I went. Even now, I ask myself why. Was it that pervasive guilt we all feel when something we are involved with, that we are responsible for, has failed? Or was I a victim? Had I always been one?

*

I didn't like the city. There was something exciting in its colour and motion, the feast of sights and sounds, the pungent smells, but for someone who hadn't worked there, it was forbidding, too teeming with life, too urgent.

The lift to the sixth floor was noiseless, and my wife's lawyer was a she, and not some smiling male assassin. Her greeting was polite if formal. Her office was large and expensively furnished, décor in varying shades of grey. She ushered me to a leather chair, stylish in her pinstripe suit, and sat on the other side of an antique desk.

I don't know what I expected. Was it Dickens? An evil-smelling Fagin with a limp or tic in some squalid room lit dimly by an oil lamp? I wasn't sure which of the two would be the more comfortable.

The papers were already on the desk. There was no need for her to explain the purpose of the meeting.

'Mr Dunn,' she began, turning the pages with her slender fingers and cherry coloured manicured nails.

I watched with morbid fascination. Each turned page was like an indictment, a passing of sentence. The air conditioning sent a breath of her Pleasures eau de toilette that hovered for a second in the air and was gone. An earring flashed gold from the sun that slanted through the window. She must have said something. I wasn't paying attention. Where was my mind? I don't think I was feeling anything. My feelings had left me. For a second or two, I wondered where I was, and what I was doing. It was so unreal.

'Mr Dunn,' she asked again, this time more gently, pointing to the last page of a document and a pencil cross, Golgotha of a doomed relationship.

I knew she understood, and I was grateful for the assumed softness of her voice, the warmth she felt was professionally appropriate.

'There's no hurry. There are a few places you have to sign.'

My hand was trembling when I signed at the first cross. The awful finality of it all. I remember wondering what she might think of my signature, and what it might say about me. So compact and legible. No wild and indecipherable flourishes.

'Would you like a glass of water?' she asked. Yes, she understood.

Moving from behind her desk, she thanked me and reached out to shake my hand. Was she sympathetic, or was it simply a resigned sadness at people's capacity to hurt each other? I was another statistic.

As I left the building, emerging from the granite and glass of high rise that muscled out the warm benignity of sky, reality still lagged. What was I feeling? Is it possible to feel nothing? Strange how a signature, even an illegible scrawl, can change a life. A second's all it takes. The decision had been made some time ago, but now it was final.

The light dazzled as I walked outside. The peak hour crowd was jostling its way home. A few passers-by seemed annoyed that I was walking too slowly or erratically. The carbon-scented air was redolent with noiseless dreams.

*

Months of loneliness followed. I'd moved to a unit in Hornsby that was near the shops, and I was able to cook basic meals. Because I couldn't be bothered, they were sometimes taken from a cardboard box.

I'd often walk around the mall simply to be among people, feeling an overwhelming, almost tearful tenderness for the frazzled mother with a bawling child, or the old man at the checkout counting copper with his rheumatoid fingers from an ancient beaded purse.

Like Lear, I felt more sinned against than sinning, and took pleasure in imagining the regret I hoped she might suffer. But apart from my pain, there was the opiate of nothingness, my senses dulled to joyless rituals.

I tried to create new routines. A regular week night for dinner with my parents. A set time to ring or meet Simon. A fierce exercise program.

I avoided the relentless incantation of divorce with all its self-justifications. Simon was caring and willing to listen, but I didn't want to bore him, and only discovered later that there may have been a reason for his interest. I was aware that most people dwell on their own innocence or nobility. I didn't want to do that. And I didn't think I could reasonably do that, even though Pam demonised me to common friends. In making me the villain, she was implicitly making herself the heroine. I suppose it's not surprising that most people always want to shift the blame.

Certain times stood out for me in that first year. One was the day a few weeks after the divorce when I returned to the house to collect some of my books. The door was unlocked because I'd told her I was coming. I let myself in, found the books and caught her hurrying naked from the shower. I was surprised by my reaction. She looked so unerotic. I felt a slight feeling of distaste, like seeing the fleshy crudities of a public change room. She was no longer part of my life. I should have been pleased. But I was saddened by it.

Another time was Christmas Day. I knew I would have Christmas dinner with my parents, and we'd exchange gifts, but I had never woken alone at Christmas. I walked to the mall searching for a silent fellowship. Perhaps a few words of cheer. A blessing. The sight of excited children with their mothers.

But it was too early and ghostly quiet. Who shops on Christmas Day anyway? The street lights were ablaze with golden sutures in the gloom. The sun hadn't appeared. I remember hurrying by an empty block where a building had recently been demolished. Broken stone hadn't been cleared. There were shards of glass. Newspapers, the crumpled news of yesterday, were zigzagging about in the breeze. So depressing! I think the demolition for me must have been a symbol of other broken glories.

Months passed. Anger lingered. Indifference grew like a cataract across an eye. And disenchantment grew with all the weaknesses we share. Human emotion seemed so fickle. Love to pain to nothingness. Yet I knew it was necessary for renewal, for moving on and building another life, possibly finding someone else. Though I thought I never would.

We're always reconstructing our own realities, revisiting what has happened to us, finding new truths, looking at things through a different lens. But it was still raw.

*

I've always been fascinated by what attracts a man and a woman to each other. What ideals and values, what complementary needs, what matching chemicals? I was at a loss to work out what attracted Simon to Grace. Though I could see why Grace was attracted to him. Am I being nasty?

An attractive nurse in a hospital must be enticing for a doctor. That's where they met. I wouldn't have picked Grace as a nurse. I don't wish to be unkind to the profession, but I didn't see her emptying bedpans or washing an elderly patient after an unsavoury accident. She was an only child of wealthy parents, and was educated at Tara, an elite school for girls. Tall, glamorous, stepping out from the pages of *Vogue*, she trained as a nurse and was appointed to St George Hospital, where Simon worked as an intern.

No need for details of their dating and marriage, but the end came suddenly in much the same way as mine had. I wasn't surprised, but needed to apologise to Simon that I'd been caught up with my own problems and should have taken more notice of what was happening in his life. He protested that he'd felt the same after my separation, and smiled saying we'd always done things together.

There were the predictable explanations Simon gave as the relationship deteriorated. The lure of marrying a doctor. Money. The spoilt girl wanting her own way and, in fairness to her, the understanding required of a doctor's wife. He later revealed that her failure to conceive wasn't a medical problem. She had never stopped taking the pill, and had been lying to him for a couple of years. Simon had wanted children, lots of them, and this discovery hurt him deeply. And it didn't do much to restore my faith in people.

And so we'd meet, often at the same coffee shop in Epping, and indulge the incantations of divorce, both of us careful not to hold the floor, so great was our need to talk and be understood.

One conversation we had over flat whites and banana bread was memorable. I can remember nearly all of it, and will report it here. It may not be literally accurate, but it's close enough.

Simon: Do you ever feel you've lost the capacity to feel?

Terry: Yes, I do. I know exactly what you mean. Didn't someone write about the anaesthesia of suffering without feeling?

Simon: Isn't suffering feeling?

Terry: I suppose it is. I think whoever wrote it, must have thought of suffering as nothingness, a void, something empty of strong emotion.

Simon: Like love, fear, admiration, hate…

Terry: Yes, like that.

Simon: I've been wondering lately if some of us are born with a diminished capacity to feel.

Terry: You don't really believe that, do you?

Simon: Why not? It makes perfect sense. We know that some people are born with less intelligence than others. So why shouldn't it be true of feeling too?

Terry: You might be right about some people never having as much feeling as others, but I don't think there's a set amount of it. Perhaps it begins to disappear to almost nothing and then regenerates itself.

Simon: Rises from the ashes? I like that, but don't you think it can disappear entirely, that you might be hurt so much for instance that it gets all used up?

Terry: You mean like a bucket with a hole in the bottom?

Simon: Yes, that's a good analogy.

Terry: And how full is your bucket, Simon?

Simon: I think my bucket's empty. What about yours?

Terry: Not much left, if anything.

Simon: Answer this then. Does the bucket empty faster when the feeling, the pain suffered for instance, is greater?

Terry: When the hole's bigger? That's an interesting idea.

Simon: Perhaps the quicker it empties, when the hole is bigger, the less chance there is of ever filling it again.

Terry: And your bucket has a really big hole?

Simon: Pretty big. And your bucket?

Terry: I think someone kicked my bucket over.

*

Three weeks after this interview, the incident at the lake with Irene took place. I didn't say anything to Simon about it even though he kept asking why I was so quiet. I'm not sure why I didn't confide. My secret would have been safe with him, though he might have tried to make me confess. He'd never tell. It might have been because a doctor is committed to saving lives and not destroying them. In retrospect, I'm sure he would have understood.

But the story isn't over yet. There's more to tell.

5

I did know why I did it this time. At least a small part of me did, a rational uncluttered part of me that bobbed about like a cork in a seething ocean. I felt no burden with what had happened to Irene. I felt nothing, except perhaps the concern about not feeling anything. No tangle of guilt and broken sleep for me.

So much of life is forgotten, lost in the murky past almost as soon as it happens. It sprints away from us so that we forget the feeling of salt spray on bare arms, the chatter of birds, the smell of jasmine, what was said that upset another. Perhaps even murder.

Had reality, even an awful reality, already become a fiction, something to put behind me, best forgotten? Anyone's death diminishes us, a poet said, because we're all involved in mankind. I may have been diminished, but I didn't feel it. It might have been that I couldn't claim to be involved in mankind.

*

Nothing significant happened in the two months after the incident at the lake. It didn't prey on my mind. My routine remained the same. Work was busy, I went running, visited my parents a few times, doing odd jobs around the house and stayed for dinner. And I met with Simon at our café, chatting as if nothing had happened.

Of all the things that could have played on my mind at that time, the one that disturbed me most was what happened with Michelle. She was a very attractive recent appointment to our legal firm. Stylish, blonde, always immaculately presented, and with a look of confidence that made you feel the world was her oyster. Some of the younger men in the firm had tried their luck with no success.

Michelle became interested in me, particularly after the divorce, and I didn't know it until her very emotional declaration. I hadn't been looking for someone, and I don't think I handled it well. She was hurt. Why disturbing, though? We find some people attractive, and others we don't. Feeling isn't always requited. That's the way things are. But Michelle was everything a man could want, and yet for me it was like looking at dry kindling that couldn't be lit.

I went to the lake because I enjoyed being there. It hadn't lost its appeal because of what had happened with Irene. I'd find comfort in the blue unblemished sky and mirrored lake, lethargic in its timeless flow and its enigmas of concealment. I'd marvel at the gum trees climbing from the water's rocky bank. And the furry wattles hijacking sun. It was the place where many of my ideas for writing were hatched.

*

Why did I do it? Why did I do it again? I know you are confounded by my inability to say why, or the lame reasons I might have given. You probably think all that background about myself was pointless, that I was fooling you, tempting you to find a plausible reason, that it was a ridiculous exercise in self-indulgence.

Be assured, I also keep asking myself why. I never stop the soul-searching. I keep asking myself why my own search for the elusive answer was oblivious to the terrible consequences for others. Why was I so obsessed that nothing else mattered? Does that make me a monster? I know your answer.

You'll want to ask me again what I was feeling this time. Nothing very much, at least when I started out. I know, I'm a broken record. Was it a means of reclaiming lost feeling?

Why Lake Parramatta? It's sometimes said that murderers return to the scene of their crime to relive the pleasure it gave them. I don't remember any real pleasure, so that can't be true of me. I knew the lake. I knew the ups and downs of the track around the lake, the bends, the watercourses, the open and heavily wooded parts. It was special for me.

Would it be too sacrilegious to say it had a certain sacred quality for me?

Who was it? Wendy. Wendy Lau was a Chinese-Australian I'd seen several times walking the lake circuit by herself. Her profile is not significant. If not her, it would have been someone else. Wendy was slight in build, flat-chested, and with straight black hair that encased her head like a dome. She lived in Carlingford, was married to Sam, a specialist in IT, and had an eight-year-old daughter.

I found out later she was a gifted musician. You'll think it strange, but details like these worried me. I didn't want to know them. It made everything more real, more substantial, in the same way words can capture feelings and thoughts, give them meaning and make them come to life.

*

I was hoping she'd be there on the Friday I had in mind. She was. I saw her leave the café and head towards the steps that led down to the lake and started the walk. She was wearing blue jeans and a pink polo top, walking slowly in a way that was almost measured, looking straight ahead. She gave the impression that exercise was the important thing, rather than a love of nature.

I would give her time before I followed. Most walkers took an hour to complete the walk, if they took the full circuit, so I knew I had plenty of time to catch her. I'd even planned where it might happen. Most of the track on the other side of the lake could not be seen, except by walkers who suddenly came upon you.

Now, I said to myself like a man on a mission. She'd been gone for several minutes, and I knew I could catch her, walking at my normal pace.

The day was warm and blue. 'Idyllic', someone later said. This time, I could hear the call of the birds, see the glitter on the lake that was losing its muddy look after a spell of dry weather.

But that wasn't the only difference. This time, I started with a purpose. There was an end I was intent on achieving. It wasn't some vague feeling like last time that became a strong unpremeditated urge moments before I struck.

I crossed the trickle of a creek to the other side of the lake, and started to walk along the gravel road. There was no sign of her yet, but I wasn't concerned. There was a long way to go.

She was eighty metres ahead when I saw her, easily recognisable from her pink top and contrasting black hair. Up ahead was the perfect place. Still plenty of time. I quickened my pace and was gaining quickly. The track had veered to the water's edge. There was a rock face behind.

I was ten metres away from her, preparing to strike, when I saw the walking party approaching from the opposite direction. They were coming around a bend in the track only fifty metres away. I hadn't heard any voices until then.

'Wendy,' one of them called, 'so good to see you again.'

And that was that. I left Wendy talking to her friends, and feeling deflated, hurried to finish the walk. There was no point continuing with my plan. Not then anyway. But I decided to try again.

I was impatient that night. Tomorrow couldn't come soon enough. I paced the rooms of my home, feeling that something had been snatched away from me. I was becoming obsessed.

She was not there the following Monday, but when I arrived on the Wednesday, I saw her in the café, and decided not to enter until she'd gone. I'd planned to go in the opposite direction, so rather than follow her, I would meet her head on. That would give me ample time to have my coffee before I had to leave. Being seen together in the café might make problems for me later.

Some people believe the weather is a portent. That if it's fine, all augurs well for what is to follow. I'm one of those people, but the day didn't reveal much. A weak sun and cloud. No rain.

I saw Wendy depart in the familiar jeans and a white top, and I entered the café. I joked with the Muslim barista about the creative design that topped my mocha. It was important that I seem natural. I left shortly after.

The track in the opposite direction falls steeply behind the dam wall and crosses a creek. I made my way across the stepping stones and up the other side of the rise to where the track widens and continues on a level with the lake. It was eerily quiet. The birds were silent. Gossamer rags of cloud were strewn across a pale blue sky.

As I walked, it didn't escape my thinking that this was to be no involuntary attack. Even if I couldn't satisfactorily explain why I was doing it, there was intent. My lame reasons I gave about Irene's disappearance no long applied.

After half a kilometre, I stopped, trying to determine if I'd been too slow or too fast over my coffee. It occurred to me that Wendy might have decided to walk a certain distance, turn around and return. Not complete the full circuit. I stood staring across the lake. I was in two minds as to what I should do. How was I to know whether she always walked the full circuit? I considered running ahead. That way, I could either meet her head on, or catch her returning.

It was then that I saw her. She was a long way off at a point where the track skirts the lake. She was coming. It was her. I lost sight of her then, but all was well. I knew she was heading towards me concealed by the many bends and cliff faces. I only had to find a suitable spot somewhere in the next few hundred metres.

As I found a heavily wooded spot close to the water, hidden from view on both sides till walkers reached it, a young man ran past me, blowing hard. Black singlet and nylon shorts. Track shoes. I heard him coming and stepped aside. Some athletes completed the whole circuit by running it.

Damn! Not again! He was the only person I'd seen. And he'd seen me, though I satisfied myself that he hadn't been looking. There'd been no greeting as he passed. No thank you. Anyway, he'd be long gone, a long way off by the time Wendy arrived.

Only a minute passed before she was with me, quite suddenly appearing from around a wall of rock. I walked towards her. She didn't acknowledge me, but stepped aside to let me pass.

I attacked, my hands around her throat. She went limp. I let go and she fell. It had only taken a few seconds. She lay still, sprawled on her back. Her eyes were fixed. And then the voices again. At first I thought my imagination may have been playing tricks, but quickly realised they were real enough.

There I was standing over someone on the ground who was badly hurt, possibly even dead. The voices were nearby. I was frantic. It was all unravelling. There was only one thing I could do.

'Help,' I shouted. 'Help. Over here, hurry.'

And as two middle-age women and a man appeared running, they could see me bent over Wendy's prostrate body in what looked like a desperate attempt to resuscitate her.

'My God,' one woman cried. 'Is she…'

'Whatever happened?' the man asked, kneeling down beside me.

'Don't know,' I said. 'I found her here. Didn't see or hear a thing.' One of the women was already on her mobile phone.

'We saw a man, in black, a young man run past us,' the man said. 'Eileen, tell the police about the man we saw.'

But his wife was no longer on the phone.

I waited for the police. So did they. They would want to talk to us. When they arrived, they heard our stories, took the necessary details, cordoned off the area, satisfied themselves that we weren't a flight risk, and told us to go, but report to Parramatta police station the following day.

I imagine you're wondering what I felt. I know you've been thinking it often enough. This time, I won't give you the same answer. I felt terrible. I felt guilt for what I'd done. I felt remorse. Even as I placed my hands around Wendy's fragile neck, and just for a second saw the startled eyes, feeling came charging back. Was it some sort of trigger? What was I doing? What had I done? But it was too late to retreat.

I didn't know what I'd expected from the experience. Catharsis. Revelation. But it was the guilt that would consume me.

We were interviewed by the police the following day. I of course deserved special attention because I had discovered the body. Sergeant

Roy was a heavy-set man with a gentle manner and a shock of grey hair. Constable El Masri, half his size and athletic, compensated for his gentleness. She was the more aggressive.

They wanted to know every detail. Did you know Wendy Lau? How was she lying when you found her? Did you move her? Did you hear anything? Would you recognise the runner in black?

I felt Roy was happy with my account, but El Masri had her doubts.

'Have you been coming to the lake for a long time?' she asked, looking at me searchingly.

I had no reason to deny it.

'A couple of months ago,' she continued, an officer from our station interviewed people in the café about a missing woman. Irene Berridge. Know anything about that?'

'We have to find that runner, Veronica,' Roy said.

It may have been the right time to confess, but I couldn't do it. Not then. If I knew my reasons, or lack of them, would be fully understood, I might have been tempted. But I knew there couldn't be such an understanding. I wonder now if it would have been any different if they'd found the runner in black. They never did.

*

A few days after the interview, Simon came to the door of my unit looking serious. My first thought was that he'd heard the television news reports about Wendy. I was named in them, and ironically my picture was shown as a good Samaritan on one channel, and a hero on another. It would have been quite natural for Simon to be suspicious.

But that wasn't the reason, and I knew something was worrying him when he said he needed to talk, and sat on the single lounge chair waiting for my audience.

He was seeing Pam, and wanted to know if I had a problem with that. He assured me that nothing had been going on when Pam and I were still married. They'd come together to support each other when both their marriages had failed, and things had developed from there.

I did my best to convince him it was all right, that Pam had a perfect right now that the marriage was over to do what she liked. He knew me better than anyone, and kept asking if I was sure. He knew it wasn't. He could read me well.

But why should it concern me? I think now that it wasn't because Pam had found herself another man. It was because of the countless hours I'd spent pouring out my heart to Simon about her. His being with her now seemed an implicit repudiation of everything I'd said about her. He'd become her confederate whether it was his intention or not.

Simon knew all this. Not much escaped him. But what could he say or do? He tried to reassure me about the strength of our friendship, its importance in his life. He said he'd leave Pam, but we both knew I'd never consent to it. My pride wouldn't allow it.

After a while, we started to speak of other things, but the talk languished. No purpose would be served to talk more. Not then anyway.

'Is your bucket full now, Simon?' I asked, hoping he didn't see it as a cheap gibe. It wasn't meant to be.

'Pardon,' he queried, not understanding.

'Your bucket. The hole wasn't too big after all.'

6

My account is coming to an end. It has probably raised more questions for you than given answers. You must have kept asking why, and I still can't answer that with any fidelity. But I do think that some things are clearer, at least for me. Do we ever know the truth?

Did I say truth? By that I mean what people are capable of, for better or worse. What makes them act in ways that are unpredictable to others, and to themselves.

I'm a different person now. I have changed over the last couple of months. I think it's for the better. I know that history won't repeat itself now. There'll never be another Irene or Wendy.

*

The guilt was terrible. I couldn't stop thinking of what I'd done, and found it incredible that I had done them. What had happened in the last months to catapult me from a state of indifference to one of remorse?

Yet I grieved equally for them both. Irene having found her feet after an unhappy marriage, decorating her townhouse, teaching languages to students who would have responded to her vibrancy, now gnawed at the bottom of the lake. Wendy, a happily married mother in her Carlingford home, no longer thrilling to the music she played, her life and the joys of motherhood snuffed out.

I thought I was going mad. I couldn't think. I lay awake at night plagued by awful imaginings. A horribly disintegrating Irene emerging from the lake and coming towards me like a zombie. A look of loathing in Wendy's eyes as she was throttled, refusing to die.

I took a week off work. They owed me time. Simon came around twice and found me deeply depressed. Our talk was friendly enough, but I know he misinterpreted my depression, thinking it was his fault, that his relationship with Pam was the problem. We said nothing about Pam.

*

The week passed, and I returned to work. Pain, whether physical or mental, usually eases with time. Mine didn't. I was a shadow of my former self. Not eating or sleeping. The remorse had overtaken me. I wondered if there was anything I could do to set things right. I could contact Sergeant Roy and confess. That would have been the honest thing to do, and I think I'd get a fair hearing from him. Not so with Veronica El Masri. But the shame would have been too great. I was a coward.

Thinking what I could do to make amends, I decided to visit the Laus. It took a few days to convince myself it was the right thing to do. It had by now been decided that I was above suspicion. As the person who'd found Wendy, I hoped the family wouldn't find it strange that I might come to offer my sympathy. I did know that it was probably more to satisfy my own need than theirs.

I stood outside their Carlingford house, a modest cream weatherboard, for fully a minute, more than ever conscious of what I'd done. I knew my visit would make everything more real, and could be painful. The house that would now be less of a home. Was it a way of punishing myself?

A broken cement path licked by kikuyu lead to the front door. As I reached for the old chrome knocker, I wondered if it was too late to retreat. But I'd come this far. An older woman, she must have been Wendy's mother, recognised me from the media coverage, seemed pleased and invited me in. There was no doubting, and not a hint of Asian reserve.

Sam wasn't home. Dawn, Wendy's eight-year-old daughter was there with her grandmother. She was a miniature version of Wendy. Petite. Straight black hair. Button nose. I felt a sudden panic, but it disappeared when Dawn, so grown-up, reached out to shake hands, and kept holding mine. I held on too. I wanted to hold her, felt a soaring affection.

I offered my sympathies as we drank Chinese tea. The grandmother was gracious, and kept thanking me. If they'd only known!

'Thank you for trying to help Mummy.' Dawn had let go of my hand so that we could drink, but was leaning close to me.

'I didn't know your mummy, but she must have been very special.' What more could I have said. 'If she's anything like you,' I almost said, but thought it might have been going too far.

'Mummy played the violin.' Dawn was becoming chatty. 'Can we play one of mummy's CDs for Terry, Granny?'

'Not just now, darling,' Granny replied. 'Perhaps next time.'

Soon after, I said a hasty goodbye, reassuring Dawn that I'd come again soon. She walked me to the door and waved before the door closed. I sat in the car and howled. I couldn't stop. I'm not sure how long I sat there. It must have been ages. A girl ran past in sporting attire, slowed and looked embarrassed, probably wondering whether to offer help, but thankfully she continued on her way.

I only just managed to get home.

*

I'm sitting on the trunk of a large tree that's fallen across the track at the lake. As chance would have it, it's at the very spot Irene disappeared. You'll have noticed that I keep avoiding the word 'murdered'. I'm writing, trying to finish this report, and this seemed the appropriate place to do so.

How do I feel? How many times have you wanted to know that? And how many times have I said I don't know? Let me answer now. Guilty but clear-headed. Remorseful yet resolute.

I parked my car in one of those prized parking bays close to the café. Removed my sunglasses. Put my wallet, mobile and watch in the glovebox, and left the door unlocked, the car keys in the ignition.

I was more subdued than usual at the café, had my mocha without the usual teasing, gave a polite wave to the curious barista, and headed for the wooden steps that lead down to the water.

I began the walk, the all too familiar walk, with a sense of timelessness. Nothing bleak. More a contented acceptance. Will people still be walking here in five years? In a hundred years? Will the same birds be warbling, the same sulphur-crested cockatoos screeching overhead? Will there be the same din of cicadas in summer? Perhaps there are some constants in a world of human flux. I hope so.

The creek that separated the two sides of the track was running, tinkling, sparkling over rock and pebble. The massive gums in this cooler hollow reached for the sun and sky.

No one has passed by. No voices this time. No interruptions. I'm grateful for that. I have it all to myself.

When I arrived at the fallen tree and clambered over it, immediately recognising the spot, I went to the lake's edge and peered into the brackish water. And there was the shelf, a metre under the water that for a few seconds held Irene's body before it rolled away and sank.

I moved back to my seat on the tree trunk to finish my writing, and sat thinking, breathing it all in for several minutes before I resumed.

The day is glorious. There's a barely audible rustling in the treetops. Three parrots just flew in front of me, their reds and greens luminescing in the sun. A couple of small lizards slid beneath a rock. The horizon's pale blue sky rises to a fathomless royal blue.

I'll finish now. The lake is beckoning.

David Reid

It is so surprising, is it not, how even the worst happenings of the past acquire a sweetness in the memory. Old harsh distresses are now merely pictures and tastes which hurt no more like itching scars which can only give pleasure now.

Ayi Kwei Armah, *The Beautyful Ones Are Not Yet Born*

1

Memory can be an act of will. Something we call on to revisit and to give us pleasure in idle moments. Or it can creep up stealthily and surprise us. I had often thought about seeing her again after all these years, and suddenly memory came like a thief in the night and wouldn't leave me alone. Punishment for my negligence. I should have made the effort to see her long ago.

She'd be an old lady now, and I knew she'd lost her husband some years before. So I imagined her rattling around in the house I knew so well, a house that must be too big now with its mementos of a receding past, and clocks that tick too loud.

I parked in the newly kerbed street outside her house, an old liver-coloured brick with a deep veranda at the front, and stained-glass lead-light windows. I was walking back into another world with faint stirrings of another life, a reclaiming of the past.

Let me introduce myself. My name is Peter. You don't really need to know more about me. My identity isn't important. I'm not Mr Cellophane, though. I have an important role, to report everything I know about the main character. And that is a lot. Growing up, we were inseparable.

Monozygotic twins are supposed to know each other's thoughts and feelings. That's how it was with us, though we weren't twins. We weren't even related. But we had the same empathy, so I feel able not only to report on certain events in his life, but to speak for him.

Opening the old rusty gate was a time warp, re-entering the distant past. The concrete path to the front door was cracked and had lifted in places. Even the doorbell saddened me, a choking sound as if it too had been infected by the years. I had to ring a second time before she answered, and stood blinking and nonplussed for a few seconds in the light before delight spread across her face. I was greeted like the long-lost son.

'Peter. It is Peter, isn't it?' she said, leaning closer to be sure.

I could smell something stale. Dusty carpet, perhaps just age.

'Yes, it is. How are you, Mrs Reid?'

'Come in. Come in. What a lovely surprise. It's been such a long time. And please call me Ivy.'

She led me to the sitting room. That's what she called it. Little had changed. The same old teak buffet with the same china ornaments, the same fly-spotted seascape, the same floral lounge, though the arms were judiciously covered with offcuts of velvet, no doubt to cover the wear, and the same table where I used to sit and play rummy with the family.

She hurried to turn off the television and move the cat from the only spare chair for me to sit. She was much heavier than I remember. Squarer. Puffing a little. The cotton print dress didn't flatter her, or hide the knotted veins on her calves and ankles. An old beige hand-knitted cardigan sagged just as she had. Her face, beneath white hair as fine as a spider's web, seemed smaller as if it had shrunk, but her eyes were kind and observant.

'I'll put the kettle on.'

I felt the years return. Always the obligatory cup of tea.

'I'm sorry, Mrs Reid, Ivy, I haven't been before,' I began, raising my voice so she could hear from the adjoining kitchen. 'But I've been thinking a lot about David recently. The past seems to gather a sweetness in the memory,' I felt the need to say. 'Even things that were once painful eventually stop hurting.'

I thought I might have said too much. And it sounded so glib. Why did I have to call on history, resurrect the past? It wasn't what I'd intended.

Waiting for the kettle to boil, she placed her hand affectionately on my shoulder and smiled enigmatically, a smile that seemed to carry acceptance more than wistfulness. 'I have so few,', she remarked, referring to the six photos she brought with the tea, and spread out in a row, face-up on the table.

*

The first was a black and white box brownie snap that showed David in his overalls, strapped up so tight they jacked his groin. At nine, his ears are sticking out, and the early moment of his 'cheese' has caught him with a foolish embarrassed look. We all know what it's like having family around for photos, watching you, urging you to smile.

In the background, the old garage sheds skin, and paspalum licks the paling fence. On the ground in front of him are birthday gifts, a dartboard, a plastic water rifle, some bags of sweets and, to the right, the bushy tail of Punch, the family dog, shooed away too late and therefore partly immortalised.

Perhaps I should start at the beginning, at least as far back as anyone can remember, except his mother. David and I were at the Reids' table playing cards when she put two photos on the table in front of me. She was laughing, a mischievous laugh, and David was embarrassed. They showed him as a baby, naked, thermal pink, his little penis prominent, probably having come from his bath and smelling of milk and soap. He looked so round and soft he would surely have bounced if he'd been dropped.

She was concerned when she realised she'd embarrassed him, but it was too late to snatch the photos away. Rescue was her only option. 'You can see him now in these,' she said without humour.

I agreed, not smiling, but looking at the faces and ignoring the plump naked David. I met him on our first day at school together. Even though we were only five, we both remember it. We both had to brave the many photos before leaving our homes. The teachers showering us with dulcet words of welcome, sing-song asking our names and patting our heads like family dogs. The mothers blinking with tears, embarrassed and laughing at their silliness. And entering our rooms in single file. I was excited. David was a little ill at ease, looking back for his mother.

I suppose the first day of school is a symbol of growing-up, moving beyond the four walls of home, facing a certain loss of innocence. I'm not sure if David's mother understood that this loss of infant innocence is a necessary and generous fate that smiles on all of us.

In those infant and primary years, we sat next to each other in class, and in the playground we were inseparable. We played with the other children, and we'd sometimes chase them as a galloping horse, with one of us upright at the front, the horse's head, and the other at the rear, bent down with arms around the other's waist, the horse's body. Years later, we'd joke about it. 'And why was I always the horse's rump?' he'd say. Not that he always was.

We'd play the usual obligatory games with our classmates. Marbles in the mainly dirt playground, tag, and catchings. In primary school years, the beanbag for catchings was replaced by a tennis ball, and handball with courts marked by chalk on the asphalt became the rage. We'd arrive in the classroom after lunch with our shoes covered in dust that we'd remove by lifting a leg at a time and rubbing the shoe on the other leg's sock.

David sometimes missed school with a migraine headache. They disappeared in adolescence but were a real concern for a young boy. Lying on his bed, his mother would sit with him, renewing the icy compress she placed on his head, and sometimes massaging his scalp.

He spoke about this often, recalling how caring it was, and how he'd sometimes ask for his special box of counters when he was feeling a little better, seeing the tears in his mother's eyes. I think she must have been moved by the humble nature of his request. Nothing sophisticated for David. He was content with his dozens of identical counters.

I wonder if this was the beginning of a dependency. David and his mother. A mutual dependency. He was an only child.

He'd often speak of the times he went to Aunt Nellie's in North Strathfield. She was a very particular and house-proud woman who lived with her father in a constant state of suppressed hostility. She was tall and slim with darting eyes and a drawn white face it was impossible to read. She felt life had passed her by.

David would laugh, saying her bony thinness suited her ascetic approach to life, a life of black and white. He liked her, but would squirm when she handed him her tweezers, and asked him to pull the hairs from her chin. Pa Rupert was a surly old man who wanted nothing to do with David, or the rest of the family, and after eating silently with them would retire to his small converted bedroom on the back terrace.

David would chat to his aunt in the kitchen as she prepared the meal, and was given a ginger ale and pink musk stick before the family sat down to dinner. Afterwards, they would play cards, Nellie's sole leisure pursuit with a group of women who'd meet weekly in each other's homes.

David would study the faces of his family as they played. His father, intent and calculating, sometimes biting his lip in concentration, his aunt with her slow release of steam in intermittent laugh, and his mother open and giving off pleasure.

Aunt Nellie would sometimes babysit when David's father had a special occasion at his lodge, and when his wife was also invited. Mr Reid was worshipful master at the lodge in Concord, which David said was very important. Next to God.

His father would be dressed in a white shirt with small opalescent buttons on the front, and a black suit. His mother would wear a long red dress and have her hair up, exposing the whiteness of her swan-like neck. David thought she was beautiful.

He remembers them returning, and his being carried half-asleep to the car by his father from Aunt Nellie's front bedroom.

We'd play together on the Reids' front veranda, a large tiled area enclosed on two sides, with a third looking over a wall to next door's yard. The veranda was a ship, plane or rocket, and next door's yard was an ocean, jungle or alien planet. We'd both take turns directing the action. The climax of any fraught adventure was stopped abruptly with no damage to the action by Mrs Reid's call for orange juice and biscuits.

At the morning teas David and I would share as adults over coffee at our favourite café, we'd laugh at the fertile imaginations we had, and how so much could be made from so little. 'If only life was like that,' he once said and laughed. Perhaps there's a moral there.

There's a memory I share with David in our primary school days, though it didn't have the same impact for me as it did for him. I've often wondered if his reaction then shed any light on the mature David's behaviour. It was a school concert. The school didn't have an assembly hall, so the children would have to walk with their class teacher down Rowe Street to the old Odeon theatre in the main street. It's long gone now.

One of the sixth-class girls was singing in pure soprano, aura-lit on stage, rarefied, the whiteness of her throat exposed. Even for me, the chastity of climbing notes still reverberates and gives me pleasure. But David was overcome. 'I'm in love,' he told me later.

He'd sometimes talk about wanting to go back to experience that emotion again, even to find out where the girl was years later.

I didn't want to go back to a hall of fetid children to find my heroine anaemic in the light and gangling in her tunic, singing out of key. And I don't want to see her again, possibly overweight and with a face that's overripe. I didn't tell David that, but he couldn't leave it behind.

Our memories are not only the record of our past, but of our identity. A defence against the forgotten years.

2

The next photo she nudged in front of me with her finger was a postcard Kodak 100 gold, that showed a pensive David near the water's edge. The sunlight is skidding on the water's ruffled foil, and softens definition. His torso is baked and lean, and his chest wears a badge of incipient hair. There's a girl beside him wearing a yellow bikini. She is pouting a theatrical kiss, showing-off to the camera, but he doesn't seem to be aware of it.

A mixed group of six or eight of us would often visit the basin on Saturdays in our later school years. The basin is a popular beach camping spot in Kuring-gai Chase National Park. We'd take the hourly ferry from Palm Beach together. There is no access by car, which is why we liked its seclusion.

There were several small beaches that were well concealed as long as you were brave enough to clamber over rocks and wade through knee-deep water at low tide. And not foolish enough to leave it too long for the tide to change, and have to swim back to the wharf where the ferry left.

Once there, we would swim, sometimes skinny-dipping, lie crumbed in the sand, eat pâté and camembert, and unwrap sandwiches we'd made at home. A few of us would bring alcohol, but most of the group, David and myself included, didn't drink. Not then.

I remember the girl in the yellow bikini because I had taken the photo. But her name escapes me now. She only joined us once or twice. I remember she had a *savoir faire*, and I suppose a sexiness in her yellow costume that was alluring for two young for their age boys like myself and David. Not having seen that photo for many years, I held it up to the light, surprised by the pensive look on David's face. Whatever was he thinking?

*

We grew together through the primary school years, and went to the same boys' high school, an interconnected series of wooden buildings in an area that barely nudged middle class. But the teachers were dedicated. We were both good students, and the democratic ethos of the school gave us both leadership opportunities. We represented the school in tennis and debating. The school is no longer there.

Leaving school, David trained to be a high school teacher of English and history. It was what he always wanted to do, and when he graduated, he was fortunate to be given a metropolitan appointment. I think it was because his father had died and he was an only child with some carer responsibilities. I also went to university, graduated in business studies, and entered the corporate world.

In the early years of his training, there were a few girls he was interested in, but the flirtations were never serious. The most promising of them was with Hilary White, a tall, reserved girl with hazel eyes and wavy light brown hair. He was smitten but never asked her out. It may be that he received no encouragement. But his reticence was the more likely reason. It may be that she felt the same, and was equally as restrained.

We'd laugh about it later over coffee, and talk about the importance of being in the right place at the right time, and of how a mumbled word or hesitant action might have changed a life. But it was another age and another culture, an age of more stylised conventions and more fragile egos.

My account of what I believe to be two of the most significant episodes in David's life as a young man comes next. I can be exact about the detail because he discussed it often, and even began to write it down when he considered writing his memoirs. The detail's important because it gives the reader insight into his feelings.

The first episode was his initial sexual 'experience'. I've recorded the word experience in single inverted commas for a reason that will become apparent later.

I was aware of something growing between David and Erin one day at the basin. Our visits there had continued over the years and David and Erin had been constant companions from the start. But there was no reason to believe they were anything more.

I liked Erin. She was a gentle and cheerful girl with a sweet doll-like face, rosy complexion and saccharine smile. Her slightly pear-shaped figure was no impediment to her clambering over rocks, or chasing frisbees.

On the day in question, I saw them holding hands. Waist-deep in the harbour water, they kissed, and on the way back to Palm Beach on the ferry, she leant against him, her head on his chest, and dozed. Something had happened that day. Fragile egos or not, they began to date regularly after that.

David would tell me about it at our regular meetings for coffee and cake. I'd be given an account of the films, the plays, the picnics and the family celebrations. He'd tell me of the desire they felt for each other, and the frustration that caused. They were both quite open about it with each other.

Before you start to condemn him for disloyalty to Erin, I need to say that there was never any attempt to impress me with his attractiveness or manhood, and he often wanted to hear what I had to say about similar experiences of mine. I gained the impression that Erin didn't mind.

David and Erin had discussed the issue of premarital sex, an anachronism now, but real enough in those days, and had decided on a plan. I didn't know about this until he told me later. They both saw sex as a rite of passage, some pseudo-reasoned way of entering the real world. They wanted to experience this together.

I don't imagine they really believed it was a way of not acknowledging a more passionate need for each other, and the part hormones played as a motive.

Her parents were visiting Canberra for three days and she was to have the house to herself. It was the perfect opportunity to implement their plan. Does that sound too matter-of-fact, too practical? Alarming? It did to me. If it had been conceived as 'let's see where our desire takes us' rather than 'let's do it because…' it might have made more sense. But to them it was like a bridge that had to be crossed.

David recalls approaching her house, a large blond-brick Cape Cod, with erotic thoughts. Not surprising. He'd been nursing them for months. He desired Erin, and the script had already been written. He'd gone to a lot of attention dressing. Neat. Casual. It was a special occasion.

He knocked and waited. A woman's prerogative. He knocked again. How would he find her? He was excited. And anxious. And aroused. For a fleeting moment, he thought her parents might not have gone to Canberra after all.

The door opened slowly. She was wearing a tight-fitting below-the-knee red dress that she smoothed over her hips, drawing attention to her ample figure as she smiled and invited him in, taking his hand and leading the way to the sofa in the sitting room.

They were uncomfortable. Talk was awkward. It had never been like that before. Again, not surprising as the grand plan hovered in the air above them waiting to be consummated. Talk of work and the weather were smoke screens. But decorum demanded at least some lead-in time. He didn't want refreshments, and wasn't to know she'd gone to some trouble. Talk lingered and died. Silence filled the room. The plan. The plan. They both knew the time had come.

David hadn't moved, so Erin shyly took the lead, kicking off her half-heels and leaning against him on the sofa with her legs tucked under her, so that her dress rode up her legs revealing a blush of white skin on half-stockinged thighs. The role of seductress wasn't familiar for the demure Erin, and she wasn't comfortable assuming it.

Instead of David's inaction cooling her ardour, it made her try harder. She may have assumed that it was her role to do the enticing.

She moved closer, her face next to his, as if she were about to kiss him, and moved her head from side to side so that her long hair brushed his face. She'd seen it done once in a movie. Feminine. Alluring. Her lips were glossed rose. Her perfume cloying. A hand massaged his thigh. The wiles of the femme fatale.

David stood, the suddenness of his movement alarming her, and without a word, rushed from the room, leaving her stunned, looking at the sitting room door as if it held some secret. She heard the front door close. He didn't return.

'Why, David?' I asked him when he told me about it later.

'It was so gauche,' he said, 'like a clumsy amateur production, too sad to be obscene.' What he was supposed to desire was denied by an awkward contrived performance. Something rehearsed rather than spontaneous.

'But isn't that what you planned?' I asked. 'Something contrived.'

He didn't answer.

*

The second episode was his meeting with Bethany. It was far from romantic or auspicious. No look across a crowded room. No orchestra. No sun or moon as matchmaker.

They met at the corner of Park and George in the city late one afternoon. She was hit while crossing George Street, thrown onto the car's bonnet, and had slid off into the gutter where she lay motionless with her head against the kerb, and one leg bent beneath her.

The elderly woman driver sat still in her car in obvious shock, having suffered a medical episode, and an impatient taxi driver blew his horn behind her, not having seen why she had stopped.

David still recalls the egg of flesh, the roundness of thigh in the torn gape of her stocking, its plumped whiteness, even in the revolving rufous lights from the police car and ambulance that were quick to respond.

He'd already hurried across the road to where she lay, not sure how he could help. Some ghouls had gathered, not bothering to go to her aid, and were watching silently, their faces muddied in the spasmodic

67

light. Most people were hurrying home, and rushed by with a cursory look as if this was an everyday occurrence.

The woman was well-dressed and appeared to be in her late twenties, though it was difficult to read her features for her face had reassembled to cope with what she was suffering. Her eyes were darting about, trying to assess the implications of what had happened. He could smell her fear.

Her arm was raised like Rodin's hand, from which there was a small trickle of blood like a macabre theatrical plot. He'd placed his briefcase of soft leather beneath her head on the kerb to afford some relief, had self-consciously pulled down her dress that had twisted around her waist, and held the raised hand.

Her frantic eyes settled on his, and tried to focus, reading her pain in his face.

'Can I do anything to make you more comfortable?' he'd asked.

She would know there was nothing more he could do. Not then.

She didn't answer, but after a brief pause she whispered, 'Don't ever leave me. Promise me,' searching his eyes.

And what surprises him even now, was his own requited response, 'I'll never leave you,' trumping every statement of feeling he'd ever made. He felt a slight squeeze of his hand as her eyes misted and closed.

The ambulance and police arrived, a fanfare of light and sound, and he was ushered away by the paramedics.

'She's not…' he began.

'Are you her husband?' an ambulance man interrupted him as she was stretchered into an ambulance. He didn't wait for an answer.

'No, she'll be all right.'

A policeman was flagging motorists into a single inquisitive lane. David still recalls a hole in the sole of her shoe, the size of a ten-cent coin, as the trolley slid away. And he remembers a strong feeling of loss as the ambulance door closed, as if something had been torn from him.

Later that night, he kept replaying her words over and over. It wasn't 'don't leave me', or even 'promise you won't leave me'. It was the emphasis given to the stand-alone promise, and the addition of the eternal ever.

One thing was certain to David even then. He had to see her. And it wasn't just a case of seeing that she was all right. What was it that had happened between them? He needed to validate the emotion they'd shared, to live the feeling that had flared so dramatically there in the gutter. It was like the feeling he'd experienced as a ten-year-old with the girl in the Odeon theatre, but more powerful. More mature. He knew it wouldn't be too difficult to find her name and that of the hospital.

In idle moments, he tried to build a picture of her life from the groceries strewn across the road from the impact, the sad accessories of simple living, the Sultana Bran and orange juice, the pair of tights and the Dove moisturiser. He tried to remember the shape of her figure, the colour of her hair and eyes.

He felt buoyant as he entered the hospital, walked past the fabric lounges and the tall vase of strelitzias in the foyer to the reception desk, and asked for the room number. At first, he'd overdressed before he decided on something less formal. It wasn't a date. 'Smart casual', invitations used to read, so he chose the beige trousers and sky-blue pullover. He'd stood for an eternity in front of the mirror, trimming eyebrows and removing ear and nose hair.

The hospital had a florist's in the foyer, and he selected a bunch of red roses, but put them back believing they implied a message that was presumptuous this early in a relationship, if there was one. Weren't red roses about deep love and desire? He exchanged them for a mix of yellow, orange and red gerberas.

He thought of the mythology of attraction at times like this, that the possibility of imminent death generated the tug of sex, some primal urge, or regenerative instinct. How many times had he heard the familiar response, usually crude yet sometimes quite serious, to the question of what you would do if you knew the world would end in an hour? The sexual urge for him wasn't the overpowering thing now. It was the intensity of his feeling, something that had been missing.

David had been thinking of little else, and had allowed two days to see that she had recovered and felt stronger. He had checked on her progress by phone, and had left his name with the hospital. Her words were an indelible magic – 'Don't ever leave me. Promise me.' – and there was the memory of her hand squeezing his as she said them.

And what was even more remarkable was the impact for him of his own words: 'I'll never leave you.' From the moment he said them, he was in awe that so much in his life was changing, that nothing could take away that acknowledgement, the rendered words that freed his guarded heart.

He hoped it was the same for her, that it wasn't just anguish speaking. Feeling hopeful, he imagined the emotion she might feel when she woke up in the hospital, and remembered having lapsed into unconsciousness on the road side, as she looked up into a stranger's caring face that held her pain. 'Ever,' she'd whispered. It was their private pledge.

She was in a single room, reading, propped up by pillows. Fortunately, there were no other visitors. He hadn't even thought of what he would do if there were. A vinyl chair was next to the bed. A vase of chrysanthemums on the bedside cabinet was surrounded with get well cards.

There was a flicker of surprise when he entered with his gerberas until recognition took over. She seemed pleased. He wanted to go to her, hold her, but thought it wouldn't be appropriate. Too soon. Besides, he didn't know the extent of her injuries, and was fearful of hurting her.

Seeing the flowers, she smiled weakly and nodded, mouthing her thanks, and beckoning him. He moved to the single chair and sat.

I have reported the conversation that followed between them as faithfully as David reported it to me.

David: You're looking a lot better than the last time I saw you.

Bethany: I should certainly hope so.

David: Do you remember it all, or is it just a blur?

Bethany: I remember it, at least till I lost consciousness. It keeps going around and around in my head.

David: Do you remember my being there?

Bethany: Yes, of course. You knelt by my side. Tried to make me comfortable. Put something soft under my head. I'm very grateful for that. It's David, isn't it? You called the hospital a couple of times, and left your name.

David: Yes. I was worried about you. And you're Bethany. Nice to meet you under different circumstances, Bethany.

Bethany: The flowers are beautiful, David.

David: I wasn't sure what to bring. I've already asked one of the nurses to bring another vase.

Silence.

Bethany: I should thank you properly. Thank you, David. You came to the rescue when no one else did. And here you are checking on me again.

David: Do you remember the things you said, Bethany? When you were lying on the road. Do you remember what we both said?

Bethany: I can't remember exactly what I said. I was in a lot of pain. But I wanted you to stay with me. I said that, didn't I?

David: Yes, you said that. You made me promise.

Bethany: Did I?

David: Yes.

Bethany: And what did you say?

David: I said I'd never leave you.

Bethany: That's so kind of you.

David: It was special. A bond. Like we were united in the most intimate way.

*

On a few occasions, David seemed to wear his heart on his sleeve. He'd often talk about feeling an overwhelming love for all people, children, the elderly, women. Particularly young women. It was so powerful, it would move him to tears. And it could be frustrating because it was inexpressible.

There were more times, though, when he feared the risky business of feeling's trade. He declared his love for me in our mid-teen years. Although frank and passionless, I asked too many questions, disconcerting him, and urging grander meaning on a simple truth. Love for me then was something definite and circumscribed, revealingly daring. Not something more general and expansive, more freely offered like it was for David.

3

'More tea?' Ivy asks with the kettle poised, and not waiting for an answer. 'This is the same one I have framed on my dressing table,' she tells me.

It's a wedding print of blown-up Kodachrome, taken at St Jude's, a small but historic stone church set in idyllic tree-studded grounds to the north-west of Sydney.

The photo has a detail crisp enough from the Leica super-zoom lens to catch the glisten of springtime droplets on damask roses held by the bridesmaids. Bethany shines in sun-added white, while David, the groom in black with scarlet cummerbund, is stilted in a cardboard pose. He looks handsome with his photogenic grin.

I don't remember anything remarkable about their courtship. There were no fiery separations and passionate reunions. They were regarded as a couple from the date of Bethany's accident, though I wouldn't have chosen Bethany for his partner.

I have long since ceased to wonder why my friends marry the people they do. To fathom such a complexity defies analysis, and is even beyond the powers of the two getting married. I remember thinking at the time that whatever the nature of the love they felt, their years together were at least a recruitment of one another to a shared version of reality.

*

Naïve and innocent, Bethany was the sort of woman men like to protect. David's part in comforting her at the accident matched her white knight romantic notions, so it wasn't surprising that she was receptive to his attentions.

Graceful, blonde, with brown eyes that nursed the world, she was the eldest of a family of girls. They were all the best of friends, though she'd left home and shared a rented unit with another girl because she thought it was important to make her own way in the world. She graduated with a degree in social work, and worked with the aged, monitoring the effectiveness of their treatment in nursing homes.

David was content. More than content. 'At last,' he said to me a few times, to signify he'd found the right girl. But he never spoke to Bethany again about the accident, and the commitment they'd made to each other as she lay on the road. Perhaps he thought it wise not to challenge the pledge unless it proved to be fragile, made in extreme circumstances.

Bethany remained in hospital for a week after the accident, and David became a constant visitor. He started by bringing her flowers, but after the second visit found she had a particular liking for chocolate. She'd suffered a broken leg, but no other serious injuries apart from sore ribs and heavy bruising.

David helped with her recuperation, visiting her at home where he was well-liked by the sisters and parents, and helping her in and out of the car with her crutches when they went to dinner, or to one of several picnic places.

Their favourite spot was Brooklyn, a small riverside settlement on the shores of the Hawkesbury River, fifty-five kilometres from Sydney. They'd often have morning tea in the café at the marina and walk along a difficult to access and overgrown bush track to a secluded beach set well back between surrounding hillside.

Walking in ankle-deep water the eighty-metre length of the beach was good therapy for Bethany's healing leg. At first, her crutch would sink into the sand and cause her to topple. They thought it hilarious. But once her crutches were no longer needed, she was hard to stop, strengthening her leg by striding in the shallows, and her mobility was quick to return.

They'd sometimes bring food from home, ham, cold sausage, cabanossi and cheese, or buy pastries at the café, and have lunch sitting on their towels and looking across the glittering water at the moored yachts and houseboats.

On a few occasions, they saw the same disabled boy near the marina café. Buses bearing the sign 'Disabled Services' would bring the children from nearby institutions, and they would have morning tea in the café. In his early teens, the boy wore a beanie that was pulled down to meet his eyes, and walked with a gait he couldn't control. His leg capered like an unheld hose.

He recognised them both and would always say a loud hello, and a halting 'I'm – going – for – a – walk,' his pride charging through the phlegmy drawl.

'Good on you. So are we,' they'd call after him.

They were quiet after those meetings. As a social worker, Bethany had to accept the inequalities life meted out. Her vocation was to help the afflicted live with them, and to achieve as much of a normal life style as possible. But David found it particularly difficult.

*

David and I met regularly at our favourite café, alter egos swapping stories of the loves that were and might have been, and suggesting panaceas for the young. We'd talk of what was heartfelt, and we'd laugh a lot.

He was happy at home, Bethany was his home, and he was happy at work. He was popular with his students, and was teaching a senior English class for the higher school certificate, a class of mainly girls. One of them was obviously attracted to him, and had made it quite obvious. Small things. Brushing past him so they touched. A hand on his arm and quickly withdrawn as he explained something at her table. Last to leave the room. Questions, only seemingly casual, about his life outside. Her classmates teased her.

'She has a crush on you, David. Be careful,' I said, suddenly serious, believing it was probably nothing, but aware of the dangers.

'No problem,' he answered. 'Good for the ego,' and he laughed.

I did too.

'She's only a schoolgirl.'

We left it at that. He knew the dangers better than I did.

I remember his pleasure the time he told me of his plans with Bethany. 'We have the house we like picked out already. Saw it in one of those home magazines. An Australian colonial with sweeping verandas at the front, four bedrooms, the main with a walk-in robe and en suite, and a study. We'll have a big backyard, big enough for two golden-haired retrievers. Come to think of it, one is probably enough, and Bethany wants at least three children, and…'

'Slow down,' I interrupted, and we both laughed. 'So it's official now, is it? Is this your way of telling me you're going to be married?'

'Of course,' he answered. 'You must have known that before now.'

'I assumed you would,' I answered, 'but you never said anything. I couldn't get excited about it, couldn't congratulate you till I knew.

'Well, you can get excited for me now.'

'I will. I am. When did you propose?'

'Not long ago.'

'David,' I began with a smile, 'that's not telling me much.' I knew him well. 'Did you propose, or did Bethany?'

'What's it matter who proposed?'

'Just interested.'

'Let's just say she made it very clear.'

'You mean she asked you?'

'Not exactly.'

I stopped the questions. I didn't want to confront him. Decisions to marry aren't always carried out with the man on bended knee before the woman, and opening the ring box to reveal the ring. That's the conventionally romantic way, but an agreement may not involve any formalities. A roundabout conversation may be enough to arrive at a contract.

The wedding was several months later. Time had passed quickly and David had been busy. The weather was glorious and the occasion was carried out in consummate style, the bridesmaids, Bethany's sisters, in flowing burgundy, and the groomsmen in grey tuxedos with white carnations.

The reception was held in a grand old mansion a short drive from the church. It had a huge dining room, and a ballroom with chandelier and vaulted ceilings. A five-piece band played a mix of old and knew, as Bethany had a large number of aunts and uncles. The dance floor was never empty. No expense was spared.

I had a wonderful time, but was ever mindful of David. It's a time when the bride and groom let their hair down. Inhibitions are forgotten. David seemed happy enough but quiet and reflective. Bethany rested her head against his shoulder as they danced the bridal waltz. She'd often spoken of wanting to do that. He also danced with Bethany's mother, and one of her sisters.

As best man, I toasted the bride and groom, avoiding both the pabulum of wedding speeches, the clichéd suggestive humour, and joking references to the fund of stories I could draw on to embarrass.

David's reply was serious, finishing by quoting Donne's valediction, likening Bethany and himself to the two legs of a compass, the fixed one defining the movement of the other, and leaning more towards the other the further it moves away.

Before they left in their streamer-decked car with its 'just married' signs and trail of empty tin cans, Bethany held me close, thanking me. 'Isn't it wonderful,' she whispered, her face beaming.

I could feel her glow beneath the slippery satin of her gown, and the rapid beating of her heart.

David shook my hand, clasping my shoulder with the other. 'Thank you for everything,' he said. 'I mean for all the years.' And then more cryptically, 'It went well, didn't it? Everything's as it should be.'

*

'You're looking at it just like I have many times over the years.'

I realise Ivy is talking to me. I've been lost in thought. Lost in the flood of memories.

77

'He was always a thinker, though, even as a little boy.' She doesn't wait for a reply. 'The day I married Frank, I couldn't keep the smile off my face. I don't know that I ever could.'

The happy couple travelled to England for their honeymoon. Travel was less common then. Most young couples couldn't afford it, and settled for a seaside resort on the coast, or somewhere in a neighbouring state. But Bethany had for many years nursed a wish to visit the Cotswolds ever since she'd read about them in *National Geographic*. David's parents were in no position to help, but Bethany's parents supplemented the couple's modest savings.

The Cotswolds are centred on the Cotswold Hills in Gloucestershire, and are famous for their tranquil old villages. They were excited and full of expectation as I drove them to the airport. David had never flown before.

They were gone for ten days. I received one postcard, but there was no point sending more as they wouldn't have arrived before their return. I heard the news of their travel later. They visited Chipping Norton and Chipping Hampden, Bourton-on-the-Water, and Upper and Lower Slaughter. They were delighted with their meals in English pubs, and nights in centuries-old inns with four-poster beds with canopies.

Most memorable for me in their travels was the last entry David made in his unfinished memoirs. It related an experience somewhere in the Cotswolds. I've read it so many times I almost know it by heart.

He set out early one morning by himself, taking a dirt path worn smooth by centuries of feet, walked past hawthorn, buttercups, bluebells, and English green. He climbed over a kissing gate that divided two fields, and had to avoid pats of horse's dung and foolish-looking sheep. He looked down on the fields below that met the ancient houses sleeping in the town.

He mentioned breathing in the efflorescence, that was the word he used, the efflorescence of the English countryside. He sat on a sawn tree stump. Said he could smell the wood sap. Felt outside time. 'Sanctified by the cathedral of the natural world' was how he put it.

Then he lay on his back in the grass, stretching out his arms and legs. Remember, it was early morning and the grass must have been wet with dew. He looked up at the pastel blue of the English sky, and felt his whole world was opening with the springtime flowers.

He finishes his account with a question. I suppose that question is what made it memorable for me. 'Is this where I belong,' he asks, gazing at the sun and moon and stars, and these are his exact words, possibly a bit jumbled, 'as the vines entwine me and the saplings root me to the earth in welcome anonymity.'

I wonder if Bethany wondered where he'd gone, or if he ever told her of this experience.

4

I'd never seen the fourth photo. It was a candid instamatic shot of three fellows carousing at a barbecue with steins raised high in mock salute, a shot that lopped a waving hand, and reddened eyes like feral cats.

An archetype Aussie male stands in the foreground and seems to be conducting a singing fest with tongs between turning meat. David, one of the three, is in the background, but he is not singing. His brooding eyes are dark like craters in a Grecian mask.

I look at the back of the photo, but there is no date, and nothing to identify the other two men. I ask Ivy if she knows where it came from. She can't remember. I assume it was taken in his early married years. Women appear to be in the background hugging wine glasses, or dangling them in impatient fingers. Bethany isn't one of them.

*

I went to a party with David once in his early married years. It wasn't my idea. He wanted me to come. Bethany was at an overnight conference, and was pleased that we were going together. She joked that it would be keeping David out of trouble. He told me he'd been to parties at this place before when Bethany wasn't available. The hostess was one of the teachers at his school.

I want to relate my experience there, not because I want a bigger part in the narrative, but because it may give a clue about the company David was keeping.

It was held in a large studio apartment in the upmarket eastern suburbs. We entered a crowded room to deafening music and cigarette smoke. Some sort of sweet-smelling smoke anyway. A few couples were dancing, but most were chatting in groups of four or five. As we threaded our way to the hostess and bar, I was aware of the repetition of 'darling' coming from every group we passed, with a drawn-out accent on the first syllable. 'Daarling'. And the laughter was altogether too loud to be natural. Everyone seemed to be chain-drinking.

The women were dressed in tight-fitting dresses exposing their legs made longer by stiletto heels, and accenting their buttocks. Their shoulders were bare, and they were heavily made-up. A few of them had enamelled young botox faces, but their lined necks betrayed them.

In a corner of the room, a not-so-young couple was pressed together, tongues in each other's mouth. I was uncomfortable. It wasn't my scene. David didn't seem to be.

One of the less ersatz women took my hand and led me to the dance floor. I was grateful that she'd taken the lead. I wasn't sure what protocol was here. She leant forward and whispered her name in my ear, but I didn't catch it. The music was loud and fast. She shook, stomped, twirled. There was no body contact. No communication of any sort.

After a couple of minutes, my partner was tapped on the shoulder and replaced by another. There were more women than men, but what did that matter when dancing was something you did entirely on your own?

'Blanche,' she said, 'and you?' She held me close, pressing, grinding her body close to mine, though the music didn't lend itself to dancing as one.

Blanche. Body-hugging, backless silver lamé dress. Long, bronzed and shiny legs. Waist-length silver hair with streaks of pink. If you think for a second that sounds like fantasy cum reality for a man, it wasn't. I could feel the dampness on her bare back, smell the vinegary wine on her breath, and see tiny grains of mascara on artificial eyelashes.

'I like you, Peter,' she said. 'You feel good.'

'Feel good,' I thought. Feel good. How could she make an assessment like that? On the basis of my being pressed against her exaggerated cleavage? Or was it just that I was the genus male?'

'Would you like to come back to my place?' There was no mistaking the message.

'But I'm married,' I answered.

'So?'

Call me a prude, but for me it was a haven of decadence. You could lose your bearings here. Is that why people came?

David was surprised by my reaction. 'That's life,' was all he had to say.

*

I remember warning David to be careful in the way he behaved with the school students, but when I heard his story, I knew what happened was beyond his control. It could have happened to anyone.

Rachel was the student he'd spoken about before, the one who liked him. The trouble began when she told him she did. They met in the corridor going to different classes between fifth and sixth period. He said he didn't know if it was by accident or design. Really, David? He does know that she very quickly looked around to see if anyone was about, and trying to make it sound casual, how's the weather today matter-of-fact, whispered, 'I really like you, Mr Reid.' She didn't wait for an answer, but turned blushing, and fled.

Words can free the trapped emotions, open the floodgates, and so it was for Rachel. The following day, she sat in class with her school uniform raised just above the knee. A little coquettish, but hardly in the same class as Blanche. She never missed an opportunity to smile when he looked in her direction.

A fortnight passed, and David was called to the principal's office, invited in, and asked to close the door. He knew this was no meeting to discuss pedagogy or senior debating. He had no idea what it was all about.

Pressed by her parents to tell them why she 'wasn't herself', Rachel had confided her feelings for David. She was upset that he hadn't responded to her remark in the corridor. You can imagine what followed.

Her parents were anxious, wanting to know what, if anything, David had done to encourage her. At first, Rachel denied he'd given her any encouragement, but she relented in the face of her father's questioning, and said she had reason to think David felt the same. She wouldn't say why.

For concerned parents, to feel the same implied some action on David's part and, anxious about their daughter's virtue, the school was contacted with threats to notify the Department of Education.

The principal was sympathetic. His main concern was whether there had been any interference with a student. That really was serious. He'd encountered cases before when a senior student and a teacher had been fond of each other. That was all right as long as nothing happened between them while the student was still under the school's duty of care.

He knew David to be one of the more likeable and conscientious teachers, listened to his story, and believed him. 'I'll do my best to sort this mess out in house,' he told David. 'I'll speak to Rachel first.'

'Then you'll want me to be present,' David said.

'No. Certainly not. That wouldn't be wise at all. And on no account try to speak to her until this is all over.'

Rachel was a shy, pleasant girl who had a crush on a teacher. She wasn't a troublemaker, she had no desire to get back at David because he didn't feel the same, and had been distraught thinking she'd made trouble for him. So she told the principal all there was to tell, confessing her admiration, but being more guarded about admitting her affection for David.

All was forgiven, but is something like that easily dismissed, put behind you? It might be for most of us, but I wonder if it were true for the sensitive David. He saw it as an attack on his integrity and his professionalism. It was an assault on a belief that was dear to him. Even with guaranteed confidentiality, word of the conflict had leaked, and David imagined knowing looks and mumblings that were probably just that. Imaginings.

I think David's ten-year school reunion also had a part to play in his change of mood. It was held in a leagues club, and boys came from all over the state, a few from interstate. David remembers looking around the room, comparing the brunt of the years, weighing the lives of the half-forgotten, feeling like an anthropologist reporting on the life span from childhood to old age, and the transition from innocence to experience, rather than seeing himself as part of the same narrative.

'It's only been ten years,' he told me, 'ten years. You could have thrown a blanket over the sameness of our lives then. Now life has unobtrusively levered us apart. What will it be like in another ten?'

He was shaken by the change. The legends, heroes and mythologies of his schooldays were no longer shared. History and culture were eating away at his precious schoolboy memories.

Most of us accept change. Even see it as desirable. I sometimes wonder if David did.

*

The phone call surprised me eight months after the wedding. I'd often met Bethany, but it was always with David. I really liked her. She wanted to meet, and gave no clue on the phone as to why. She didn't want David to know of our meeting, and I saw no disloyalty in that unless our talk was to become a personal attack. I didn't think David had any secrets to hide from me anyway. We met in the same café where David and I used to meet.

Bethany hugged me, and sat down. We ordered and waited for the coffee to arrive. Her hand shook a little with the first sip. I waited for her.

'Can I ask you some personal questions, David?' she began.

'Of course you can, Bethany. Anything you like.' I wanted her to feel comfortable. Hoped my voice sounded warm. Besides, my life was an open book.

'You'll know I'm talking about David.'

'Yes. I suppose there's no avoiding that.'

'How do men show their love, their feelings? It's different for men, isn't it?'

It was a simple question that didn't call for a learned answer. It was a way in to something more personal.

'I think it is, Beth,' I answered. I could already see where this was heading. 'I think women are better at it than men. Probably always have been. They express their feelings more easily. I'm not sure why. I think men of our generation learned that it was sissy to show the softer feelings.'

'Like love?'

'Yes, like love, and tenderness…'

'And you, Peter? Is it hard for you?'

'Perhaps not as hard as it is for David.' I immediately regretted that answer, though I didn't think it was such a revelation. Or betrayal. It was where she wanted the talk to go. 'It doesn't mean he doesn't feel those things,' I added. 'Only that it's hard to put them into words or act on them.'

'I sometimes wonder, Peter…'

I knew the important question was coming. 'Wonder what, Beth?'

'Wonder if he feels for me as much as I feel for him. I tell him what I feel, but he doesn't answer in the same way. I say "I love you" and I don't get the same response. I go to him for a hug, and I know he really enjoys it, but it's not very often that he comes to me.'

'Have you spoken to him about it, Beth?'

'Yes, of course. And he assures me I'm the most important thing in the world for him, but it doesn't make much difference. Has he said anything to you, Peter? Only tell me if you think you can.'

'He talks of you often, Beth. Keeps saying how lucky he is to have you.'

'But does he say he loves me?'

'Yes,' I answered instantly, before I thought about it. I reckoned he did, but it wasn't a word he used as freely as I did. I wondered later if I'd ever heard him use it. But for Bethany, the seed of doubt was already planted, and I wasn't going to water it.

She was pleased by the answer and seemed reassured. I knew it wasn't right to ask about the more intimate expressions of feeling. It might upset her, and whatever they were, I could predict the answer anyway. 'That's different,' she'd say, and I suppose it is.

She left happier than when she'd arrived, and I felt I'd played my part well, for both of them. I'd answered her questions honestly, possibly with one exception, and I'd been loyal to David. I could see that she feared the peril of her own acknowledgement, that once she became convinced that her suspicion was real, her fears about his lack of feeling, the deluge would begin.

David was so open with me, full of the joy of life, but he always seemed to be searching for something more. It was only when I saw this photo with its brooding eyes that I recalled his cryptic and matter-of-fact assessment of his wedding day. 'It went well, didn't it?' 'Everything's as it should be.' Odd? I think so.

Was love for him circumscribed? Did he always have to keep something in reserve, a cache for days that would never come, a natural inclination to love, yet a circumstantial will against it?

5

I'm surprised she kept these last two photos. And she didn't have to go rummaging through drawers. She found them immediately. They were obviously well-thumbed and must have been a constant reminder. Surely they could only promote unwanted memories.

The Fuji colour print had been torn into jagged halves and sticky taped together. The crumple in the gutter is unmistakably David. It was the early hours of the morning, but the flash thyristor control has lit a face that slants with shuttered eyes to the brook of ochre vomit congealed by the winter chill, and a shirt tail flags the open trouser fly where an empty amber bottle has rolled.

I fetched David from the gutter. A well-meaning passer-by found my business card in his wallet and phoned me. He waited there with David till I arrived. I don't know who took the photo, or how it ended up with his mother. I only hope it wasn't someone trying to hurt her with some moral lesson. But I do know that I was the one who tore it in halves.

*

The marriage failed. Most people have a theory about failed marriages, a theory that's often reducible to a single cause. And that cause is usually the fault of one of the partners. That's a naïve view. They usually look for symptoms, but a symptom may not explain causation. It may be the result of a far more deep-seated problem. I think most marriage breakdowns are not the result of what someone has done, or hasn't done, but who we are. Perhaps there's some clue in these wandering thoughts of mine.

When Bethany called, speaking in almost a whisper, I knew the writing was on the wall. She needed to talk. Would I mind? I didn't have a problem with seeing her before, but now it was different, and I wondered if I should see her at all. I knew David would confide in me and tell me his side of the story.

I was in a difficult position. I couldn't be seen to be taking sides. The role of mediator was one that could lose the friendship or respect of one of them, if not both.

I knew where my loyalty lay. I had to be David's advocate. But I didn't have the heart to say no to Bethany, and I knew she wouldn't knowingly put me in an awkward position. And I didn't think David would object anyway.

We bought takeaway coffee and went to a nearby park. She didn't want to talk in the café again. That was a warning in itself. We sat on a wooden bench and finished our coffees without saying a word, watching the young mothers taking their children to the park playground. It was hot and blue and magpies sang, not a fitting backdrop for what was to come.

'I'm leaving him, Peter,' she said suddenly.

'I thought that was coming,' I said after a long pause.

She hadn't expected me to be surprised.

'Where will you go?'

'Back home.'

There was a longer silence this time. The news had been given, and she may have been thinking where to take the conversation from here.

'Was David happy?' I asked. 'I mean, was it his decision too?'

'Not really.' She made no attempt to dry the tears that had started to flow freely. 'He agreed. Well, he acquiesced, I think that's the right word, isn't it? He said he didn't want me to go, but said it might be for the best.'

'He didn't plead for you to stay, argue with you, promise things would get better? I knew what David felt for you.' I stopped. Was I already trying to mediate?

'No…not much anyway.'

Not much meant not at all. There was another silence. She was waiting for me to take the lead. I knew she needed to say more.

'Do you want to tell me why, Beth, why you're ending it all? It's so…final.'

'It's hard. I knew what I was going to say. Now I'm not so sure.'

'You were talking last time about David not showing you any affection.' She needed a prompt.

'That's the main thing. I don't know how many times we've spoken about it, but it's never any different. Sometimes, I think I might be pushing him, asking him for something he can't give. I feel I'm nagging, but I don't feel I'm being unreasonable. How hard is it, Peter, to show you care with some loving words, a caress?'

'Is he cold with you?' It was my turn to push. I felt she couldn't say he was.

'No, he's gentle enough, but…' she searched for a word. 'Distant.'

I needed to know more. 'Do you have any reason to believe that he doesn't care, doesn't love you?'

'If you love someone, wouldn't you want to show it? Wouldn't you have to show it? I mean, wouldn't it be beyond your power to resist showing it?'

What more could I say? We're all so different. Some of us are extroverts. Some of us are introverts. Some are puritanical and some are pleasure-seekers. And some of us are less demonstrative than others. Bethany had a need for more open demonstrations of affection than David could give. I had no answer.

'You mentioned the main thing, Beth. Are there others?'

'I think he's disappointed in me, Peter.'

I was surprised. More than surprised. 'But he's always saying how wonderful you are. I find that hard to believe. Why would he be disappointed?'

'I believe it all goes back to the accident.'

'The accident? Where do you get that from?'

'Peter was there for me, helping me as I lay on the road. In a sense, he rescued me. He was the white knight on his charger. We both shared the same romantic feelings about the rescue, about helping. When he visited at the hospital, I fell in love with the white knight.'

'And he fell in love with the lady fair.'

'Did he, Peter? Did he? Or did he fall in love with the idea of the lady fair? Was the real me disappointing for him?'

I had no answer, though I could accept her theory about David's romantic attitudes. He was often lost in the clouds. She shrugged when I asked her if it was a trial separation, saying that the problems had never gone away, so why would they now.

I was wary about meeting David because I knew he'd want to know if I'd seen Bethany, and what she'd said. It put me in an awkward position, but I decided to report in full what Bethany had talked about, and be careful to avoid giving an opinion or advice. That's what I did.

We met at our usual café, where there was a table outside, distant from the others. The waitress could see there was an urgency about the meeting and kept her distance. Conversation may have been a little more strained than normal. We talked a lot about marriage and the problems people face. There was little humour. The only discussion I remember clearly is David's answers to Bethany's concerns.

'David, is it what you want, for Bethany to go?'

'No. It's the last thing I want. I'll be lost without her. She knows that.' He was sitting forward with his head in his hands.

'Did you tell her that? I'd imagine she'd have loved to hear it.'

'I told her I didn't want her to go. Isn't that enough? She knows how I feel about her.' He was a little irritated by my question, probably because it touched a raw nerve.

By that point in the conversation, I was finding it hard to keep to my resolution of not judging or giving advice. 'David, do you think it might have been the right time to plead with her, to tell her you love her, or at least to tell her you don't want her to go?

'Sounds simple, doesn't it, Peter? Let me try to explain. Bethany's great, but she always wants more. She's always asking what I feel about her. She's very loving, I give her that, but whenever she tells me she loves me, she gets upset if I don't respond by telling her the same thing. Whenever she gives me a hug, she sometimes says it would be great if I gave her a hug. Even if she doesn't, I'm expecting her to say something. I'm on tenterhooks all the time.'

'You think that's too much to expect?' I tried to keep my voice neutral, not to colour it with what I really thought.

'Perhaps not, but I find it suffocating. There's never an end to it. If she'd stopped and allowed it to happen, to come naturally, I might have…'

'Might have given her what she wanted, what she needed,' I finished the sentence for him.

He nodded. I had trouble believing him.

Then as if he had read my thoughts, 'I could have done more,' he said glumly.

I said nothing. Such a bald statement might give some room for negotiation, but if he knew that, why hadn't he done more?

'You know Bethany thinks her accident was significant in your coming together?' It was time to change direction.

'She told me what she thought about my romantic attitudes and my supposed disillusionment in her that followed. And she asked me if I thought that was true.'

'How did you answer that?'

'I told her it was ridiculous, and I might not have been very nice saying so. It is ridiculous. Talking of the accident, I wonder, Peter, if she felt obliged to keep the commitment she made lying there in the gutter. "Don't ever leave me," she said.'

'You think she married you to keep her commitment?'

He just shrugged, probably because he saw the reaction of disbelief I'd hoped to hide. I'd tried to be impartial, but how could I be? Bethany married for love. I had no doubt at all about that.

I've seen it so often, particularly at times like these, times of conflict when people feel they are under attack. They rework something that's happened to show themselves in a more agreeable light. Massage it. Distort it. Even make a fiction out of it.

David was becoming withdrawn. It was time to stop. 'She's probably right,' he said. 'To go, I mean.'

My annoyance with him changed instantly to sympathy. I wanted to reach out to him, but what could I do? This was at least an acknowledgement that he wasn't easy to live with.

It was a sad day when Bethany left. There was no bitterness. Just the opposite. She packed her car with her clothes, books, a brass they'd bought and her personal effects. Barnie went too, the imitation dog that slept on their bed with them. David was miserable, standing by the window in the front room, watching her come and go. He offered to help, but there was little he could do. I stayed with him as Bethany made several trips to the car.

The most poignant moment wasn't when her car pulled slowly away from the gravel driveway. It was when she stood in the doorway, whispered goodbye and hugged David. She looked at me for a split second. 'Look after him,' her eyes said. At that moment, I felt as if the world was upside-down. I can only imagine what David felt.

After the failure of his marriage, we drifted apart. When he was with Bethany, we'd meet every month, swapping our stories of juvenile loves. From the worldliness that comes with age, we ridiculed the inhibition of those years, sharing our memories while sipping coffee and flirting with the waitresses.

Our meetings may have become less frequent, but our friendship remained strong. The pressures in my own life were one reason for less contact, but you don't need to know about them.

I looked at the photo on the table more closely. It had been years since I'd seen it, but some images print themselves on your mind indelibly. The empty amber bottle. I didn't know he'd started to drink. I'd never seen him have more than a glass or two. There was never any evidence of it when we met. I suppose you don't get a prize for guessing when that began.

David remarried a year after his divorce. It came as a complete surprise. Bethany had tried to help him through a difficult period, encouraging him and taking an interest in his teaching. She even mothered him, but there was to be no reconciliation.

His second wife Faye was very different from Bethany. Highly intelligent, plain, with mousy-coloured hair, she scorned the world of image and appearances. She graduated in medicine, and completed one year of her internship before abandoning it.

I found it hard to believe that anyone could complete six years of medicine and relinquish it so easily. David told me there'd been a hiccough during her internship, and Faye could not cope with being a failure in anything.

The wedding was a strange affair, conducted with virtually no ceremony. I was the only one of David's friends there, yet Faye had invited her friends and her extended family. There was no reception, at least not one I attended.

Faye was controlling and protective, protective of herself and not David. She insisted they live with her parents, though did agree to them having separate accommodation. David paid for renovations to her parents' house.

I've never understood why David went along with Faye's rulings. Was it simply a matter of wanting to keep the peace?

Within a few months, there was physical abuse, and although Faye was the abuser, once attacking him with a frying pan, she was the one who called the police, accusing him. David suffered the indignity of being grilled. Physical abuse was more the province of men, so David was given a hard time. Fortunately, the police believed him.

It's no surprise that the marriage ended in less than a year. David lost heavily. I hadn't seen him in this time, and we quickly renewed contact. But it was a different David.

*

Sometimes, I saw his decline as one of those unpredictable happenings that life throws at us. At other times, I felt guilty. Could I have done more? Said what I really thought he should do in his marriage with Bethany? Counselled him against his bizarre second marriage? But there's no golden rule about when to interfere. Friends are supposed to bear each other's challenges. Had I failed him?

David had once unlocked the feelings that I never thought legitimate between men. The feelings that were once only sparingly spoken to women when the lure of romance beckoned, and that often resulted in injured feelings and game-playing, were replaced by the deep and sexless bond of male companionship that toughens when there's threat. The feelings I once confessed to David were to another self.

6

I don't know how she came to be in possession of the final photo, or who might have taken it. Perhaps it was a copy of an official police record. The towers of Circular Quay float upside down in this Konica print, and a lunchtime crowd fly spots the pier for a glimpse of the body that bloats a snarl of drowning garden rubbish and the plastic detritus of sex. From a heeling launch, two policemen are using grappling hooks with the passionless mien that reminds the onlooker that this is just another day's work.

I didn't hear of his death for a few months, and still remember the shock. It was Ivy who had contacted me. She had apologised for not getting in touch earlier, but said that when the news came, she'd had a nasty turn and took a long time to recover.

Death, even if it is expected, is bewildering in its impact because it's hard to accept the sudden passing into nothingness. Looking at the photo now, the pain of that first revelation returned. I could feel the blood drain from my face, as it had then, and found myself studying the photo as if I needed proof, some evidence that it was David in that snarl of rubbish, or that I might see some tiny overlooked detail to shed new light.

The hardest thing to accept was David's reason behind it. The police were quick to establish that there were no suspicious circumstances. I was never interviewed. The circumstances of his recent life spoke for themselves.

To welcome death, you have to be glutted in heart, mind and spirit. Sated. Why couldn't he have turned to me? I felt guilty that he hadn't. What hurt me more than anything was the thought that what we shared had been disintegrating with the rest of his life. The death of anyone is always the concern of those who are left behind.

*

We finish our tea in silence, and she's the one who rescues me. I realise she's been watching me closely. She could see the effect the photos had, and quickly gathered them, putting them in her apron pocket.

'Ivy, are you…' I begin.

'It was all such a long time ago,' she interrupts, 'and before you ask, yes, I'm all right. I play cards with the girls twice a week, and I go to Probus. I get a bit lonely some nights but I have the TV and Snuggles.' The cat is purring loudly on another seat.

I leave with promises of returning soon that I'm determined to keep. I have to wait for the slice of carrot cake she carefully wraps in foil with arthritic fingers. The rusty gate squeals as I close it behind me.

The world beyond the gate seems larger than ever. Small children playing next door, and a friendly dog that bounds towards me, compete with my inward-looking thoughts.

My memory is the only shield I have against the killjoy of the fleeting years. Its preservation is a record of both my history and identity. Sometimes, I wonder if my many memories of David and myself are just the same as his were, or whether some are fiction, made more real when thinking makes them so.

Do memories always disappear with age, or do they multiply, exaggerated by the wisdom of our creeping years, to fit the meanings that we've come to prefer – what did I say about massaging circumstances? – or to sustain the hope that looks forward rather than backwards?

*

It's his turn to order and pay. It's always the same, a large flat white for him, a mug of mocha for me, and a pear and raspberry bread we share.

'Make the mocha really hot,' he tells the waitress. He knows me so well.

We're in our favourite café where so much has passed between us. There's a smile on his face. A twinkle in his eye. He's telling me a funny story about something that happened at his school. We both laugh.

The waitress, a girl of eighteen we know well, brings our coffees.

'You look particularly attractive today, Sophie,' David says.

'And so do you, Mr Reid,' she answers, equal to his flirting.

'What about me, Sophie?' I protest teasingly.

'Even more attractive,' she says with mock feeling.

'Aaww,' David groans, pretending injured feelings as she walks away.

'She really thinks you're the more attractive,' I say. 'I was just a diversion, to make you jealous.'

'I know,' he says.

We laugh. This is part of our mythology.

Phillip Steadman

None but a coward dares to boast that he has never known fear.
Ferdinand Foch, attributed

To know what is right and not to do it is the worst cowardice.
Confucius, Analect

1

He'd been exercising his whole life and was determined to keep it up. It started at school when he needed to be fit enough to win the cross-country. Then it was because he wanted to look good for girls. Then with his maturing years it became a mediaeval ideal, strong in body and in mind. Now, in middle age, it had become the means of staving off stroke, heart attack and other illnesses.

He regarded exercise as a panacea. Not so much a cure-all as a pre-ventative. He knew there were some things exercise couldn't prevent. He'd already lost a few of his contemporaries to cancer, and some had been as fit as he was. Yet modern opinion seemed to suggest that after eliminating drinking and smoking, exercise was the next best thing to do to preserve your health.

There were even studies claiming that exercise helped in stalling de-mentia. They had really struck a chord with him because his own father had the disease. He remembers his mother shaving him, chatting like she always had, and dabbing shaving cream on his nose to nurse the pretence of a joke. Cutting his breakfast toast in easy bites and making sure his tea was lukewarm in a half-full double-handed mug. Fetching the bleach to clean the shower from a not-so-pleasant accident. Lying next to him in bed and feeling his unresponsive warmth as her memories zigzagged off like butterflies. And then her insistence that he would not go to a nursing home. All of these medical problems had an impact on others as well. If exercise could do anything to keep dementia away, it was a small price to pay.

He was thinking all this as he put on his Reeboks. But it wasn't the only reason he went running. He felt better for doing it. Exercise was supposed to release endorphins and give a feeling of well-being. He kept telling himself that when he came back exhausted.

'Don't overdo it,' she warned him. It was the advice she gave every time he went. 'You're not a young man any more.'

'But better than most,' he answered as he headed for the door, not wanting to be reminded of the creeping years. It was good advice he didn't heed. I never do things by halves, he used to tell her. She knew that only too well, but this time he said nothing.

It was a five-kilometre run beginning outside his house with a kilometre climb before the path levelled for a few hundred metres and entered a long narrow park with bush on either side. Exiting the park, he'd follow the broad sweep of footpath past the small cluster of shops and head for home making sure he ran on the nature strip to save his ankles.

It was early morning when he began the climb beneath a constipated sun that peered through rags of morning cloud. He passed a runner coming from the opposite direction. A familiar face. He waved. His heavy breathing eased as he entered the park. It felt good to be away from the traffic, to be on level grass and have this strip of nature to himself. Sometimes, he timed himself using familiar markers, a towering but dead gum tree not far from the entrance, a grassy hollow, a large boulder. But not today.

But he didn't have the park to himself. In the distance, he saw two men, perhaps three, in a tight-knit cluster. What were they doing so close together? Was it a game of some sort?

As he approached them, it became clear. Two of the men in dirty army fatigues were beating the third. His head rocked backwards as he was hit on the side of his face. The victim, older and well-dressed for work with a shock of sandy brown hair, had a surprised look on his face that changed to one of pained non-comprehension as if the act needed an intelligible explanation. It seemed the aggressors and victim didn't know each other. So it was either robbery, or the desire to hurt for the pleasure of it.

The victim's briefcase was reefed out of his grip by one of the men and thrown into nearby bushes, and, trying to get up from the ground, muddied by the early dew, he was twisting, trying to shield his face from the kicks.

The two men saw the runner approach, now only thirty metres away, but didn't stop. One stared at him from a scarred face, probably a legacy of previous assaults when he wasn't in control. And smirked. A look that was surely an invitation. Do you want some too, it seemed to say.

He was shocked, his indignation at such an outrage tempered by fear, a lack of breath, possibly from jogging, and a heaviness as if his body was flaccid and unable to move. But worst of all was the feeling of powerlessness, the indecision. What was he to do?

The two men continued to kick the man on the ground, deaf to his pleading.

*

'You've pushed too hard again,' she admonishes him when he returns from his run. 'You look done in. I keep telling you.'

He's standing on the porch, bent over, hands on his knees, and breathing hard.

'Is everything all right?' she asks, suddenly concerned, and moving towards him. 'Do you need a glass of water?'

His eyes are adrenalin-wide, and there is a slight hint of foam around his mouth.

'Sit down,' she orders, leading him to the swinging seat on the porch, and is about to go to the kitchen for the water when he starts to speak.

'Two hooligans,' he begins, and needs to take a deep breath. 'Two hooligans were beating up a man.'

'Where?' She's really concerned now.

'In the park.'

'Whereabouts in the park?' She wants details.

'What's it matter whereabouts in the park?' he nearly answers, but doesn't. 'They saw me running towards them, but they didn't stop. One punched him in the face, knocked him down, and the other started kicking him when he was on the ground.'

Now that he's freed the words, they begin to flow, a haemorrhage of indignation. 'Late teens, early twenties, shaved heads, piercings, tattoos, really rough looking. I'd recognise them again. They smirked when I got nearer, as if they were daring me…and they didn't stop.'

'You mean they kept kicking him?'

He nods, pauses. A loaded pause. He wants her understanding. It wasn't a pleasant experience for him. Perhaps a few words of comfort. But she says nothing. She's waiting for him to continue with the expected sequel. The silence is unnerving.

'What did you do?' she asks impatiently.

He hadn't expected that, and instantly realises he should have. What did he expect? Perhaps a concerned enquiry about what happened next, or whether the two thugs were going to attack him, and not something quite as confronting.

'What did you do?' she asks again. She wants proof of his nobility, or a courage that doesn't count the cost. 'They saw you running towards them, you came up to them, and they didn't stop. You surely didn't let…' she asks again, and reads the answer in his face.

His importuning eyes confuse her allegiances. Her sympathy for him is trumped by something stronger.

'I probably saved his life,' he defends himself, aware of how hollow it sounds. 'They stopped soon after that.'

The lame bravado falls between them heavily to settle like a quilt.

'How soon after that did they stop? Did you stop and watch while they beat him half to death? Did you run by as if it were just another run?' Her feelings are obvious now.

He doesn't answer.

'You said they stopped. What happened to the man? Was he left lying on the ground seriously injured?' There's a longer silence as she allows her disappointment time to settle. 'I'm getting the impression you don't know what happened to him. Only last night,' she resumes, 'we were talking about this very thing, the need to educate children for a better world, the need to rid the world of violence. How many times have you and I spoken about it?' Her wearied feeling dies, and the clichés wither on her tongue. And as though he has been guilty of a great hypocrisy, 'You were always our great apologist!'

She leaves the porch without another word, and retreats inside the house, making him feel like an accomplice. The air is heavy with recrimination.

His feelings are ambivalent. She is right. He could have done more. At least try to appeal to the men or threaten them with the law, look menacing, or stay behind to see if the man needed help or medical attention. How hard is it for a man to admit he's scared?

But what did she expect him to do? The man with the scarred face would have welcomed the opportunity for him to join the fight. His look said as much. Did she expect him to wade in boots and all? What if they had a knife? A gun?

They'd certainly had many talks about their vision of a better world where there was no place for violence. Was she being the advocate now of something she deplored? Did she want him to try to stamp out violence by becoming violent himself?

He decided to ask her these questions, but when he entered the house after her, his son was at the breakfast table.

'Good run, Dad?' he asked. 'Did you do your best time?'

'Get your bag, darling,' she said quietly. 'I'll drive you to school today.'

And leaving for his school bag, even at the age of ten, his son was aware that something wasn't quite right.

Once his son had left the room, he went to her, reaching out, wanting to hold her, but getting no response. 'One thing's for sure,' he said, 'next time I see them, they'll get a thrashing they won't soon forget.'

In the cider light outside, the orb of sun retreats behind a cloud.

2

There are usually times in every life when people look back over the struggle of the years to consider where they are now, and feel well satisfied. They might even do so feeling gratified, believing that they have earned the contentment they enjoy from their own efforts.

Others give silent thanks, knowing that their comfortable lives have been decided by forces beyond them, and that it could have been otherwise. And there'll always be those who won't ever feel this peace, either because life is unkind, or because they'll always find something to complain about.

Phillip and Leonie Steadman were humble about the way things had turned out for them through their own efforts. They lived in a comfortable house in a good suburb. They were regular churchgoers. The mortgage was manageable because both of them worked. They had Toby, a ten-year-old, who was happy at school, and little trouble at home, and they both enjoyed their work as teachers, Phillip as a high school teacher of English, and Leonie as a fourth-class teacher at the local primary school.

If they'd been asked whether or not they had a happy marriage, and one of Leonie's friends did from time to time, they both would have answered with an unequivocal 'yes'. Of course they were different, every couple is, but they found their differences endearing rather than irritating. Comments like 'he has to be on time – hates being late', and 'she has absolutely no sense of direction', were always conferred lightheartedly, and usually followed by laughter, and further teasing.

At thirty-seven, Phillip was sandy-haired, blue-eyed and of average height. A few admirers said he had a strong face, and he often wondered what that meant. His childhood sensitivity and aesthetic sense had grown with him, disciplined by the insights of maturity.

His father, a self-made man from leaving school early, was an accountant for a large organisation. He carried the residue of his own Victorian parenting, but he was reasonable and kind. His mother worked as a secretary in a government office, but only when Phillip and his younger brother were both old enough to go to school.

He did well with his studies, regarding himself as talented but not gifted, and earned a scholarship to train as a teacher. He'd always wanted to teach, having played 'schools' in his childhood, though teaching for him then was more about power than pedagogy.

At thirty-five, Leonie was the middle child in a family of seven children. Her father, a celebrated old boy of a prestigious private school, sent his four sons to the same school. It was a loving if male-dominated family, and Leonie learned to serve, though it was more because of her generous nature than any family pressure. She had an unusually strong relationship with her mother, who ran her own small business to supplement the family income. It was apparent from an early age that she would find work in one of the service occupations, helping others. Nursing and teaching were the obvious choices. She chose the latter, underwent training at the Catholic Teachers' College in Strathfield, and was appointed locally to teach fourth class, a grade she'd been teaching at the same school since her appointment.

How many loving relationships begin with outright hostility, only to mellow into something loving? Theirs did. Few would call it romantic. Their first meeting was unfortunate. A car accident. They were both driving home from their respective schools. A waste disposal truck was emptying bins and taking up most of a lane. Leonie, heading in the same direction, squeezed past but, in doing so, had to cross the middle line by a metre or so. She'd looked to see what was coming towards her, but hadn't seen Phillip. They collided. The damage wasn't great, but both cars needed significant repairs. The waste disposal truck kept going as Phillip and Leonie parked their cars.

'You must have seen me getting by the truck.' Leonie was angry. It had been a frustrating day at school.

'I didn't see you,' Phillip answered. 'The truck blocked my view.' He wasn't going to tell her he'd been thinking of how to be a triffid in teaching Wyndham's novel to Year Nine.

'How could you not have seen me? All you had to do was move over, and not hug the middle of the road.'

'All you had to do was be more careful in checking oncoming traffic.' Phillip didn't appreciate the criticism. She was blaming him.

'I did. I stopped and waited before I eased out.' She was gesturing wildly and there were tears of anger and frustration. She knew the law was on his side. She had crossed the lane line. But he must have been half-asleep.

He knew that he was in the right, at least technically, and was annoyed by her refusal to accept the blame, but he kept quiet.

They were strained as they exchanged insurance details and phone numbers in case there were problems, and left. Both cars were driveable.

After they'd both settled things to their satisfaction with their insurance providers, he felt the need to contact her, not because of any attraction, but because he didn't like the altercation they'd had, and thought he might have handled it better. She felt the same, finding it hard to believe that she'd blamed him, and welcomed the call so she could set things right.

'My mind was elsewhere,' he told her. 'I was thinking about how to motivate my students.'

'I was at fault,' she answered. 'I was in a hurry and should have waited for one of the garbos to wave me past. What are you teaching?'

And so it began. They started to see each other, and the relationship grew. In three months, they were engaged, and in six, they were married. Years later, they'd look back on the accident and say it was the only serious disagreement they'd had. Until now.

*

'You should have seen him today,' he tells Leonie trying to show enthusiasm he doesn't feel. He's just returned home from collecting Toby from his weekend cricket, and the incident in the park is weighing heavily on his mind. Or rather Leonie's reaction to it is.

Toby is excited and bright-eyed, and Leonie stops chopping bacon at the kitchen bench, and prepares herself for the blow-by-blow description.

'We won, Mum,' Toby can't wait. 'Thirty-four not out. My highest score. Mr Munroe said I can bat at number five from now on.'

'He was terrific,' Phillip pats him on the shoulder, 'and that drive through mid-on to the boundary, that was really something.' He's trying hard to please one, and appease the other.

'That's wonderful.' Leonie forces a smile. 'We're proud of you, Toby,' she adds, looking with fondness at the little man in her life. She'll ask him to set the table for their dinner guests later. To do so now might seem to be a penalty.

The Lathams and Hunts are regular dinner guests. The Lathams are happy-go-lucky, fun to be with, and their very bulk seems to lend heft to their undiluted views on any topic. The Hunts are more reserved, some might say more refined, and both Phillip and Leonie sense something amiss in their relationship, some disturbing undercurrent. Paula Hunt is the one who asks Leonie about the happiness of her marriage. Leonie is wary of revealing anything, and of returning the favour.

The talk begins with questions about work, dominated by the men. Paula is a legal secretary with a pale aquiline face and a mole on her nose. She has cropped dark brown hair. Julie Latham is a platinum blonde who aspires to be chic by wearing skimpy clothes designed for eighteen-year-olds. She doesn't work.

Once the lamb rack arrives, and the wine is poured, the talk moves to issues.

'How's the law?' Phillip asks Paula. It's a facile question but that's often how large-group conversations begin.

'We're both lucky, Phillip,' she answers. 'There'll always be children to teach, and there'll always be people doing the wrong thing who need prosecuting.'

'And people who've done nothing wrong who need defending,' her husband retorts.

Paula's displeasure is obvious.

'My father used to talk about sins of commission, things you do that you shouldn't do, and sins of omission, things you should have done but didn't,' Julie contributes, feeling she has made a worthwhile contribution.

'Not the same thing,' Paula says, never missing an opportunity to show her superior knowledge.

Phillip shifts uneasily in his seat.

'Like seeing a murder and not reporting it.' A swarthy Bill Latham rescues his wife.

'Doesn't have to be as bad as murder.' Paula picks up the thread. 'Seeing theft, seeing assault can be prosecuted.'

'Talking of assault,' Geoff Hunt wades in, 'do you teach the kids at school anything about dealing with violence?'

Phillip explains the relevant section of the personal development curriculum dealing with respect for each other. Leonie is watching him closely. The buffoon in Bill Latham focuses on domestic violence, suggesting the need to keep women in their place, and is shushed by Julie.

When they have finished the lamb and mint sauce, Leonie goes to the kitchen to prepare the sweets, and is joined by Paula.

'Tell me if I'm wrong, Leonie, but is everything all right?'

'Yes.' Leonie is surprised. 'Why wouldn't it be?'

'You can tell me to mind my own business, but Phillip seems a little distant, not his usual self, and I had the impression that there's a coldness between…'

'Can I do anything to help?' Julie enters the kitchen, and sensing she might have walked in on something, wonders if she should retreat. Paula frowns. Leonie is pleased she'd come. It just might have saved her from telling Paula what she suggested, to mind her own business.

'Why don't you let me do the clearing up,' Phillip tells her when the guests have gone. You've done enough.' He's still trying to win her favour.

'I think that went well,' Leonie says, an hour later. She hadn't left Phillip to do the clearing up alone. 'They liked the lamb and mint sauce.' She is standing semi-naked beside the bed as Phillip undresses.

They lie down together.

'Do you think Paula is happy with Geoff?' Phillip asks. 'There's something, I don't know what it is.'

'I don't think they're happy at all, and haven't been for a long while,' Leonie answers, and is surprised it has only just occurred to Phillip. She is tempted to tell him that Paula thinks the same about them.

'You did a wonderful job tonight,' he says. 'The perfect hostess. The meal was great.'

His fingers walk his hand across the bed sheet to find her, and come to rest against her hip. There is a quick reflex movement as if she's been stung, and she rolls over to face away from him.

*

'It says on the back cover that the theme or main idea of the book is forgiveness. What does that mean? Jess?

'Telling someone it's all right if they've done something wrong.'

'Good answer, Jess. Is that all?'

'Not holding it against them.'

'And why should we do that? If they've done something wrong, shouldn't they be punished?' Leonie's trying to provoke them, make them think.

'A little. We all do wrong things, Miss Steadman.'

'Yes, we do, Amy.'

'But can you punish and forgive, miss? Aren't they different?

'Excellent point, Scott. What does everyone think?'

'If someone's done something really bad, they should get some punishment, miss, and then we forgive them.'

'You're saying, Charlotte, that every bad thing has consequences, but we can still forgive?'

'I think I'm saying that, miss.'

'Miss, if the person who's done a wrong thing is really sorry, doesn't that make a difference?'

'What do you think, 4S?' Brett's saying that if we own up and are sorry for something we've done, it might be easier to forgive us.

(Chorus). 'Yes, miss.'

'Do you think that's the message of the story? What the author is trying to say?'

'Yes, miss.'

*

'"This above all, to thine own self be true." Think about what it means. Think about who's saying it and to whom. It's one of the most famous quotes by Shakespeare. Greg?'

'Polonius says it, sir.'

'And who's he saying it to? Kirsty?'

'Is it Hamlet, Mr Steadman?'

'No. It might have been, Kirsty. It might fit with the play, but it wasn't Hamlet. Anyone? It's just the sort of thing your dad might say to you. Yes, Todd.'

'Laertes, sir, his son.'

'Yes, and why did he say it?'

'Wasn't it because Laertes was going to university, and he wanted to give his son some advice?'

'Yes, Sue. What do you think it means?'

'That we should only do things that we believe are right.'

'Excellent, Sue. Anyone else? Bruno?'

'Do things that are like…like what our real nature is…but that's what Sue said.'

'No, perhaps there is a difference there, Bruno, between what we think or believe, and what we do, or who we are as a person. Has anyone found it yet? Yes, Sarah. Read it out.'

'"And it must follow as the night the day, thou canst not then be false to any man."'

'Anyone? Melanie?

'If you're true to yourself, like honest with yourself, then you'll automatically be true to others around you.'

3

Leonie refuses to admit that anything is wrong, at least to Phillip, but a shadow has been cast over the relationship. It isn't her intention to punish him, but It's as if she has withdrawn into her shell, that some of her earlier *joie de vivre* has been scrubbed away.

She continues as she has always been, doing what she has always done, but something is missing in how she behaves with Phillip. She is attentive to him, or at least she goes through the motions. At times she is animated, and some of her signature cheekiness returns, but it seems as though she is fighting her gloom, determined to stop it from taking over.

The change in Phillip is even more marked, his depression more obvious. He has always been sensitive to Leonie's moods, and knows that she has become withdrawn because of him. If only he hadn't gone running that morning.

He becomes easily frustrated when students are refractory at school, when a task at home gets the better of him, or when his computer doesn't behave. As the weeks pass, he puts off the Lathams and Hunts on more than one occasion. Leonie's in no mood to see them either.

After a fortnight, during which the incident has been ignored, he confronts Leonie. It doesn't start as a sane talk that becomes hostile. It starts angrily, and takes her by surprise. They have just sat down in the living room after dinner. Toby is upstairs doing his homework.

'Tell me, just tell me,' he nearly shouts, 'what do you think I should have done?'

Leonie is so shocked by the outburst, she doesn't reply before Phillip resumes. It takes her a second or two to realise what he's talking about.

'Would you have been happier if I'd come back with my front teeth missing, a few broken ribs and a bunged-up eye, or,' and he becomes so aggressive that Leonie begins to cry, 'perhaps a broken arm or spine. Well, I'll tell you something, if I'd done any more, I would have! If it'd been Geoff Hunt, he'd still be running away.' He's facing her with his arms by his side and his hands clenched.

He does apologise but worse is to come. They'd eaten late one night because of a school staff meeting that Leonie had to attend, and when they'd finished the meal, she asks Toby if he would do the washing up, his rostered night to do so.

'When I've watched my show, Mum,' Toby answers.

Phillip leaps from his seat, shouts, 'Don't you dare answer back,' and slaps Toby across the face.

The silence is palpable. Time is frozen. Seconds pass. Only faint canned laughter comes from the television in the family room, mocking the real-life drama.

Leonie is horrified, and looks from Phillip to Toby and back, her mouth open, before she moves to Toby and holds him. Phillip's anger is gone as quickly as it arrived, and he too looks shocked as if he's only just realised the meaning of what he's done. He's standing looking helpless, mortified.

To add to Phillip's misery, Toby, his eyes filled with tears, turns to him, and says, 'Sorry, Dad', before Leonie whisks him away.

Phillip sits in a heavy silence, never having felt so forlorn.

Later that night, he creeps into Toby's room to apologise. Toby is lying on his bed, pale-faced, reading a cricket book, still shaken. He's never been struck before, but is relieved that his father is no longer hostile.

Phillip sits on the bed next to him. His apology is not half-hearted. 'What I did was unforgivable, Toby,' and he pauses. 'There's no excuse for that. It won't happen again.'

'All right, Dad,' Toby answers, not certain that he's done anything wrong.

'How about a half-century on Saturday,' Phillip persists, trying to return things to a cheerful normality.

'Sure, Dad,' Toby replies without enthusiasm. 'Why don't you go and see that man in the hospital. The one who got hurt?'

Phillip is bowled over by his son's percipience, but reckons it couldn't have been his idea. Leonie must have explained why he'd been behaving differently, tried to soften the literal blow he'd suffered. They must have spoken about what could be done to help him.

He does go to the hospital. The name of the victim makes it more real. Graham Nicholson. Small-business owner. No longer a faceless victim. Identifiable flesh and bone, lying there in his striped pyjamas and wire-frame glasses, probably loved by a wife like he is. Might have a son like Toby.

Phillip takes chocolate and magazines, some that aren't too lurid. He's already formed an image of Graham Nicholson, a conservative well-dressed, possibly colourless man.

Graham is grateful for his visit, and understanding when he explains his part in the drama. He doesn't lie, but he doesn't tell the whole ungarnished truth. He tells of how he hurried over as the men were finishing beating him. Well, they were nearly finished. He doesn't say he scared them away, and he definitely doesn't say they took no notice of him. Graham says he was only half-aware that someone else was there, and thanks Phillip for his intervention, saying it might have made the difference between life and death, and that he'll buy him a drink when he's on his feet again.

Phillip's talk with Graham makes a difference to his spirits. He'll tell Leonie what Graham said. It might help restore some of her faith.

*

For a week after the incident with Toby, things between Leonie and Phillip are strained. Leonie knows that Phillip is remorseful, but the sudden flaring of his temper disturbs her. This is a man she doesn't know. Phillip had spoken to her before he apologised to Toby, and his obvious distress softens her reaction. She holds him, but not with any conviction. That image of the slap, and Toby's bewilderment and pain is frozen in time.

'Please, never...' and she doesn't finish. She doesn't have to. The message is clear enough.

Phillip is attentive to them both in the weeks that follow. He was always a big help around the house, and now he doubles his efforts. He secures the wobbly leg on the kitchen table, paints the third bedroom and fixes the chain on Toby's bike.

Toby does score a half-century at cricket, and that, with Phillip's praise, goes a long way to restoring the bond between them. He insists on taking Toby to the mall for his favourite ice cream sundae, and buys him a book on Bradman.

He hasn't been intimate with Leonie, though he desperately wants to be. She isn't dismissive or cold. She gently asks him to give her a little more time, and takes his hand, cuddling up to him as they lie in bed talking of the day's happenings. At least it's a start.

And time does make a difference. Leonie starts to overcome her feelings of withdrawal. She realises that Phillip needs the support that he's never asked for or needed before, and that he's always given her. With that knowledge, she becomes more responsive. Things haven't returned to normal, but progress has been made.

She also recalls an incident when she was new to high school and was bullied in the playground by older girls who called her names and pushed her around. No one came to her aid. She's been wondering if this has coloured the way she reacted to Phillip's meeting in the park. She is well aware that our beliefs are refracted through our own experiences.

One Saturday afternoon a month after the incident, when life has all but returned to its halcyon days, Leonie, paying for her goods at the supermarket, hears shouting from the car park where Phillip is waiting for her, and recognises his voice. She hurries outside to see Phillip berating a bellicose-looking man in his forties, and standing close to him in a threatening manner.

'Who the hell do you think you are?' the man snarls. 'It's none of your bloody business.'

'It's everyone's business,' Phillip shouts back.

The man's wife stands by his side, looking timid and very uncomfortable. 'Please go,' she says to Phillip tearfully. 'Please.'

A small crowd is gathering, and Leonie, not wanting her husband to make a scene where she shops at least twice a week, pulls him away. He leaves reluctantly, observing the wife's pleas, and realising that she might pay for his interfering. They drive off quickly.

Once home, Phillip explains that the man had been belittling his wife, telling her she was useless, calling her dirty names, and that he'd pushed her so that she bumped her side on the bonnet of their car. He'd intervened and, yes, he had threatened the man.

Leonie isn't pleased. Phillip may have intervened when a woman was being maltreated, but there are some situations it is better to ignore. The man couldn't have done anything more serious in such a public place. He may have been right in telling Phillip it was none of his business. There were other more appropriate courses of action. Yet the similarity with what happened in the park is not lost on her.

Her real concern is Phillip's anger. Even in the telling, he is becoming agitated, and this persists throughout the night. He can't let it go.

Phillip is sceptical of the psychologist they visit together at Leonie's insistence. He needed convincing but had to agree, particularly after the incident with Toby, that he was getting too angry. And he had to consent or Leonie would think he wasn't facing-up to the problem, and all the good would be undone.

The psychologist is pleasant enough, a dark-haired balding man with a Jewish nose, sitting back in his leather studded chair, hands together, fingers interlocked, listening to Phillip's account of witnessing the attack on Graham, and speaking of the impact of stress and anxiety on the brain that can lead to the production of stress hormones and the possible loss of memory and ability to reason.

Phillip becomes impatient when he speaks of the need to talk to friends and not isolate himself. He calls it 'grounding exercise', the need 'to be validated'. It is the sort of common sense Phillip tells his Year Eight students.

Leonie and Phillip do listen more attentively when he outlines a typical chain of feelings following an incident of the sort he has experienced: assumptions like failing to cope, underlying feelings like powerlessness, negative perceptions of self like feeling inadequate, leading to negative perceptions of others, and finally antisocial behaviour. He seems particularly interested in Phillip's guilt.

'Well, I'm not sure where that got us,' Phillip remarks as they drive away. But he doesn't want Leonie to feel discouraged, and he's pleased she's heard a likely profile from the psychologist that may help her understand him. 'He's probably right,' Phillip tells her, 'about the negative perceptions of myself and therefore others.'

Leonie is pleased that Phillip has admitted the visit might have done some good, and is interested in the psychologist's focus on his guilt.

*

'You haven't been yourself lately,' Tim Matthews, the sixth-class teacher tells her, sitting down next to her in the staffroom with his pie and sauce from the school canteen.

'Is that right, Tim? Who have I been then?' Leonie had hoped her change in mood hadn't been noted at the school.

'Clever Leonie. I'll tell you who've you been. Mrs Glum.' This is the name of a reader third class use.

But Tim is showing concern. Other teachers have noticed he's shown a lot of concern ever since Leonie came to the school.

'I suppose you're right, Tim. Sorry. I've been a bit distracted.'

'Everything not going as it should be in paradise?'

Leonie is aware that Tim's concern is coloured by a curiosity that she finds uncomfortable. She's sometimes wondered about his reasons. 'Nothing serious,' she answers. And to divert his attention, 'Not in paradise anyway.'

'A few of us have noticed, Leonie. You know what everyone thinks of you here. We're all concerned.' Tim has realised that he might have overstepped, and is now making it a general concern.

'Tim, I really appreciate that. I know you care, and I'm grateful. It's good to have friends like you. She means it.

'I know it's a throw-away line Leonie, but if there's anything I can do, you only have to ask.'

Several other teachers enter the staffroom, and sit beside them. Leonie is relieved no further personal talk is possible, and Tim adopts his 'hale-fellow-well-met' stance with the other males.

*

'You said the man at the supermarket was being horrible to his wife.' Diane leaps to Phillip's defence. 'Don't you think he should get a pat on the back for that?'

'But there are ways of doing things, Di. It may have been a good thing that he intervened to protect the poor woman, but it was getting nasty. He could have said what he had to and walk away. But he was so aggressive I thought it would erupt into a fist fight.'

Diane is Leonie's best friend and confidante, a self-assured and slim, blue-eyed blonde who has kept her figure by working on her fitness. Their friendship started at school and continued through Diane's messy divorce and miscarriage. She works in the private sector and lives alone in her own two-bedroom unit.

'You're right, there was no need for a shouting match. And the poor man's wife might suffer for it when they get home.' Diane feels the need to show her allegiance.

'And then the incident with Toby. For a moment, I hated him, Di, really hated him, seeing Toby in tears, but when I saw how stricken he was, I was tempted to protect him like I was doing for Toby. Go to him.'

'It's not like him,' Di sympathises. 'He's such a gentle man. I suppose we can all lash out suddenly, a moment of madness, and regret it. But Leonie, you said you spoke to Phillip before he apologised to Toby. That was your chance to set things right. Give him a hug…or whatever it takes to set things right.'

'Now you're being naughty.' She smiles. Diane always knows when to introduce lightness into a serious conversation, to relieve the tension.

'No, I'm not.' Di is quite serious.

'Di, that whole business in the park did upset me. I'm not sure now what I expected him to do…something more, or something different. You'd think it would have been easy for me to get over it, but you behave in a certain way, he reacts, and then you react…'

'And it gets out of control. With every passing minute, it gets harder to reclaim what you had.'

'You know what I mean. It's like the ripples a stone makes when you throw it in the water…ever-widening circles.'

'And the water can get muddy. Excuse the mixed metaphor. Leonie, I sometimes look back on my divorce with Roger, and wonder if one of us had made a stand before it all became too much…to stop the escalation.'

'That's where I am now, Di, but it's easier said than done. So much has happened since then. Thoughts take over. They eat away. Defences spring up. Doubts and self-doubt. Someone becomes hardened or inured.'

'Leonie, you joked, accusing me of being naughty. But might that be an answer?

'Possibly. It sounds so simple, doesn't it? It's not, and I'm not sure that he wants that any more, whatever I feel about it.'

'You don't think he'll do something now? Come to you, ask you to put it all behind you. From what you said, he did try early on.'

'Yes, I think he did. I know it's up to me. I blame myself, Di. It's my fault. Is there anything worse for a man that having his manhood attacked? I accused him of not doing enough, when he might have been hurt if he had.' She starts to cry. 'And then I turn around and stop him interfering with the man in the car park.'

They're silent for a minute, both steeped in their own thoughts.

Di is the first to speak. 'A fresh start.'

'Sorry?'

'You need to make. Fresh start.'

'For us both. Go on.'

'Have Phillip move out. Don't look so alarmed. Not permanently. A week or two. It's probably the best thing for both of you. Time to think without the other around. Time to realise how important you are to each other. And when he comes back…no more ripples. There'll be no end to the naughtiness.'

'He'd never agree to that. Where would he go?'

'He could stay at my place. Better than having him go to a hotel. I have a spare bedroom. I could keep an eye on him for you.'

*

Leaving home from a marriage would normally be painful. Perhaps there'd be a chilly silence, or harsh words spoken. There might be fighting over what is taken, or even one partner standing sadly at the window while the other drives away with a wave of regret.

That wasn't true of Phillip leaving. There was no wailing and gnashing of teeth. Leonie had been surprised at Phillip's reaction when the plan had been suggested. After several seconds of silence, he said it was a good idea, and saw it as an adventure. Leonie had been dreading suggesting it, and was relieved when he agreed without a moment of doubt.

He left on a Saturday morning, wheeling the case he used for travel to the car. They'd told Toby a believable story about his brief absence. Leonie came with him to see him off, thinking she'd ring Diane as soon as Phillip left. It was so ironical that his imminent departure had lightened things between them, so much so that she wondered if his going was necessary after all. What would Diane think? She even harboured thoughts as to why he was so cheerful. Was he so eager to get away? Did he find the thought of being with another woman appealing? Not that she had any concerns about Diane's motive.

'Make sure you tell the Lathams and Hunts that we've separated,' he joked.

Leonie pretended to shudder. 'And cop a million questions from Paula. Or have Geoff make a play for me. I don't think so.'

She stood facing him to say goodbye for a couple of seconds before he opened the car door. Neither of them made a move to the other. She regretted that she didn't, and felt a little empty as Phillip drove away. It seemed such a good idea, but she was the one who'd be alone. More ripples in the stream.

4

Diane lived in a neighbouring suburb in a block of six honey-coloured units in a tree-lined street. She'd been there for six years, her former house having been sold as part of the divorce settlement.

She welcomed Phillip enthusiastically. 'This is my humble abode,' she said, leading the way inside. 'I'll show you where to put your bag.'

Phillip carried his bag so that its wheels didn't mark the carpet, and headed for the main bedroom. 'Well, I suppose this is my bedroom,' he said, looking at the double bed, the flowered doona, the pink dressing gown hanging on the door, and the clutter of cosmetics on the dresser.

'Out of bounds, Mr Steadman,' Diane replied smiling. 'Your room's across the hall. And if you don't like it, there's always the broom closet.'

'How big's the broom closet?' he asked with mock seriousness.

'If I move the brooms and vacuum cleaner out, you might be able to sleep standing up.'

'Perfect,' Phillip replied.

He put his bag in the second bedroom, and joined her in the living room. There were pastries on the coffee table. He was already enjoying himself. He'd never been here before but he'd always liked Diane.

'Just so I know what I have to do to help, you might tell me my responsibilities.'

'Well, I thought that you could take responsibility for the shopping, cooking, cleaning, housework and taking out the rubbish,' she said, imitating his seriousness.

'Fair enough,' he said, 'and what will you do?'

'Every place needs a supervisor,' she answered. 'I'll sit here and see that things are done properly.'

This tone was characteristic of their relationship for the next few days. Phillip couldn't do enough to help, and when Diane took his arm on several occasions and led him away from the kitchen sink, or took the vacuum cleaner from him, he'd answer with 'But miss, you told me…'

'Miss will smack your bottom if you don't behave,' she'd say, to which he'd answer, 'Yes please, miss.'

They enjoyed each other's company, would experiment with the cooking, and sit together after dinner and talk. That was preferable to television. She told him details he hadn't known about her divorce, things she'd told no one, and found a sympathetic ally. He told her about the incident in the park.

She wanted to be loyal to Leonie. She knew how Leonie had reacted to Phillip about his behaviour in the park, and didn't want to say she didn't agree. But she told the truth. 'It's very difficult to know what you could or should have done. I don't think you could have charged in boots and all. They might have killed you. Perhaps you might have…'

Diane, living alone, was a creature of habit. Up at seven, and lunch at twelve thirty if she were home. At eleven, she'd go to bed. So would Phillip, each to their own room.

One evening, they decided to go to the local cinema. They discussed whether they should, whether Leonie would like it, whether it crossed some line, and decided that it was perfectly natural for two friends to see a movie together.

There'd been no other man in Diane's life since the divorce, though there'd been no shortage of admirers, and she was surprised by being excited. She dressed a little more stylishly than usual for such an occasion. So did he.

'I feel like I'm dating again,' she said, searching for her handbag.

Phillip was enjoying it too. She was an attractive woman, and she seemed to understand him. Talk was easy. She took his arm as they walked the few blocks to the cinema. And they relished the date, choosing to behave as they might have years ago. Choc-topped ice creams and popcorn. On the way home, they held hands and ran the last block, she in her half-heels, laughing. Phillip wondered what his students would think of him.

Their date brought about a subtle change. The light-hearted banter didn't disappear. But a gentle concern grew alongside it.

'I feel like an old married woman,' she said. 'Perhaps I shouldn't say it, but I've really enjoyed our time together.'

'So have I, Di. I hope you meant a happy old married woman, and not one who's grown bored and sick of her husband. Has Leonie said anything to you about when I go back?'

'No, we didn't set a time, but it can't be long now.'

The following night, they had a special dinner to mark the end, or near-end, of their time together. They debated going to a restaurant but preferred to stay at home.

'I'm cooking,' she said, and because it was special, they both dressed in the same clothes they'd worn to the cinema.

Phillip bought white roses to place in the centre of the table. They lit a candle.

After dinner, they sat on the lounge together. They had their set places now, and began to relive the last six days together, sometimes laughing, sometimes wistful, sometimes teasing. She took off her shoes and snuggled up to him. He put his arm around her and she kissed him gently on the cheek.

'It's been great,' she said, breaking the silence. 'In the last day or two, I wondered if it's been a good thing or not…feeling as I do.'

It was no time for Phillip to be light-hearted. 'I've felt the same, Di,' he answered, holding her tighter. 'But you must think it's been a good thing. I do.'

'Wrong place, wrong time, Mr Steadman. You do know, don't you, if Leonie wasn't my best friend, and if you were available, I might be inviting you to my bedroom right now. There are some etchings there that might interest you.'

'You mean my bedroom, don't you?'

'You wish.'

Leonie saw them enter the cinema. Diane was holding his arm and they looked like two excited children. Why were they overdressed? It gave her a surprise, made her feel a little uncomfortable. Yet they looked happy together, and there was nothing wrong with her taking his arm.

The whole point of the exercise was for her and Phillip to start afresh. It was only natural that if he was to live with Diane, share accommodation, that is, they would sometimes go to places together. There might be a difference between going to the shops and going to a movie, but he could hardly stay locked in the unit when he wasn't at work. So there was no need to worry. Nothing was going on between them.

It had been four days, and she'd heard nothing from either of them. Diane had said she would keep an eye on Phillip. That surely meant reporting in. But then again, what could she report…that he was unhappy, happy. That wasn't the point.

Phillip hadn't phoned, but no arrangement had been made with him about contacting her. He might have assumed that it was to be a complete break for the week, or however long it was to be. Or his attentions might otherwise be engaged. Something might be going on between them.

Di was her best friend, which should make her above suspicion. But why would a single woman suggest that a man, a handsome man, move in with her? Was it an attempt to win her husband's favour under the guise of helping out her ailing marriage? And Diane wasn't just attractive. She was stunning. She'd expected Phillip to oppose the plan, but he accepted it straight away, and he was excited about going. Something was going on between them.

She rang Diane believing she might be able to tell from her voice if there was something suspicious. She'd know. Call it a sixth sense.

Diane seemed pleased to hear from her. 'It's going well this end,' she said light-heartedly. 'How is it with you?'

'Everything's fine.' She tried to sound upbeat. 'But I thought you were going to report to me.'

'Of course I'll report, but I didn't think you wanted me to do so throughout the week. I can if that's what you want. I don't know what I can pass on yet. Your husband is a gem, Leonie. He's a big help around the place. If things were a little tense to start with, he's certainly relaxed now. So from what we planned, it must be working.'

Leonie didn't learn anything from the call. Diane seemed pleased to hear from her, and was open about everything. No evasiveness. So she returned to the feeling that something might be going on between them.

She met him returning from shopping the day before Phillip was due to return. He was a couple of blocks from her house, and sitting on the kerb with his head between his legs.

She didn't normally address strangers, but he seemed to be in some distress, and he was well dressed. He was certainly no ne'er-do-well. 'Excuse me,' she asked tentatively, 'do you need help?'

'No, I'm fine, thank you. It's kind of you to ask. I felt faint for a minute. Just taking a breather, getting over an injury.'

'Let me help you home. Do you live far away?'

'It's quite a way. I try to do a long walk every day.'

She wasn't sure why she made the offer. He seemed a gentle man, light-coloured eyes, green or perhaps blue, and light brown hair, con-servatively dressed. 'I live two blocks away. Why don't you come back? You can have a rest if you need to, a cup of tea.'

He came with her, protesting that he didn't want to be any trouble. If she was in two minds, so was he.

'No trouble at all,' she reassured him and they continued in silence.

Reaching the house, she became more doubtful, considering whether she should invite him inside. Was she tempting fate? She had the car keys. It would be simpler to drive him home. She wondered if her loneliness this last week had something to do with it. But if he'd been faint, a cup of tea with plenty of sugar might be the answer. She did invite him in, and she did make him tea.

'Here I am,' she said, handing him the sugar bowl, 'serving a strange man tea, and I don't even know his name.'

'I'm Graham,' he answered. 'And you?'

'Leonie.'

'Well, it's very kind of you, Leonie. I appreciate it.'

'Are you feeling better now? You said you were recovering from an injury.'

'Thank you. A lot better. Yes, multiple injuries. A few weeks ago, I was mugged in Boronia Park.'

Leonie felt the blood drain from her face. It's him, the one Phillip helped, or didn't help. She wanted to ask him about it, see what he remembered about a stranger who came upon the men who were assaulting him. But he'd be sure to wonder about such specific questions.

'Do you want to tell me about it?' she asked, hoping he might give the details she wanted to hear.

'No,' he answered. 'I've relived it so many times now. I'd rather forget it.'

She didn't want to tell him her husband was the other man. Perhaps he knew more about it than he'd told Phillip in the hospital. He might be nursing resentment. That wretched incident had caused enough trouble already.

She has no clear idea of how things happened after that. She does remember what finally happened. They made love. She'd look back in disbelief. He was too proper to have made the first move, and she was too dedicated to her marriage. Why then? Was it her acid feeling that something was happening between Phillip and Diane? Could it have been in some bizarre way she was repaying him for Phillip's lack of action in the park?

She remembers them undressing, he hesitant, she like the sacrificial lamb, standing, waiting. She remembers the clumsy grappling, limited by his injuries, his white hairless chest, thin arms, the determined face above her, the time and effort it took as though it might have been difficult for him.

And then him dressing hurriedly in silence, was he ashamed, while she lay on the bed naked and not attempting to cover her ravished body

– well, hardly ravished – his 'I'd better go,' and the door being closed so quietly it didn't make a sound.

She didn't get up but lay there looking at the ceiling. Why? It wasn't just loveless sex. It was lustless sex. It had meant nothing for either of them.

5

When Phillip returned home, Leonie was pleased to see him, but she wasn't demonstrative. She was still anxious about the time he'd spent with Diane and whether anything had happened between them. She'd decided that as soon as Phillip arrived home, she would ring Diane, ostensibly for thanking her for looking after Phillip, but to probe about the time they shared together.

There was another reason for her not being demonstrative. It had only been a day since her affair with Graham. She grimaced at the word 'affair'. Might 'encounter', 'collision', or even 'misfortune' be a better word to describe it? Whatever word might be used, the action it stood for was relationship-ending, the conventional reason for marriage breakdown.

But how could it have meant nothing?. Even for it to happen, emotionless and passionless as it seemed to be, there must have been some need to be satisfied. That worried her. What need was it?

She felt guilt. Convention frowned on it after all. But who would believe her glib defence that it had meant nothing? 'At least a moment of weakness,' they'd say. And it was certainly that.

She argued with herself about telling Phillip and quickly decided some things were better left unsaid. It would achieve nothing and could only cause harm. She thought of confiding in Diane, but if anything had happened between Diane and Phillip, it might come back to bite her, be used by them against her as a means of pursuing their own ends. The easiest thing was to say nothing. It was nothing.

Those were her thoughts as she rang Diane.

'He's back, Di. Just wanted to thank you and check how it all went.'

'You tell me, Leonie. How was he when he got back? I thought you might be…you know, celebrating.'

131

'You're being naughty again, Di Travers.'

They'd already returned to their light-hearted banter. That was a good sign.

'And why shouldn't I be? I think it went well, but the proof is how he is now, with you.'

'He was pleased to see me. We hugged.'

'And?'

'Give us a chance, Di.'

'What did you both get up to?' Leonie regrets it as soon as she's said it. It might imply getting up to no good. Diane is astute enough to read between the lines. She knows she could have worded it better.

'That sounds ominous.'

'I mean what did you do? Your typical day.' Leonie realises this is what she should have said in the first place.

'Breakfast together, work, took turns cooking dinner, then talk half the night over a glass or two of wine…and we went to the pictures once.'

'So you really got on well together?' She is relieved by Diane's honesty about going to the cinema.

'We did. He's great.'

'Not tempted, Miss Travers?' It was time to return to their usual light-heartedness.

'Of course, Mrs Steadman…but he's my best friend's husband.'

The call dismissed Leonie's suspicions. There was nothing to suggest Diane had anything to hide. She didn't conceal their going to the cinema, and she didn't hide liking him. She talked freely about what they did, and their sharing. It was only natural that she like him. As her best friend, it was desirable that she did. Within limits of course.

With the understanding that they hadn't cheated, her guilt about Graham resurfaced. And she felt poorly about suspecting them when she was guilty of the very thing she condemned.

Was it fair that you should be branded by the act, one silly act, and not the feeling that went with it? She would put it behind her. It was one sapless indiscretion. Yes, that was the word for it, indiscretion. She didn't want to be poisoned with the pen of adulteress. Already it was becoming remote, as if it had never happened.

She would begin now devoting herself to Phillip. She had, until recently. All this had sent a message. She loved him and no other.

*

She did devote herself to Phillip. She had always been unselfish and attentive, but now she was more so. She tried to anticipate his needs and was even more affectionate than usual. It concerned her that she baulked at any further intimacy, but only did so because she felt it was too soon after Graham. She needed to put a little time between the two men. So she played the role of temptress, told him she wanted to have a special dinner to celebrate, and then, 'Well, my love, I'll leave it to your imagination.'

Phillip had been understanding. He sensed the change in his wife and was pleased with how loving she was. He knew it was only a matter of time before they'd make love. He'd enjoyed his time with Diane, and could see that the purpose for it had been realised, for both of them. He was probably closer to Leonie now than he had ever been.

Leonie had never given him the third degree about his time with Diane. She'd been satisfied with his accounts of what they'd done. He admitted to liking Diane, but stopped short of mentioning the temptation they'd both felt on that special dinner night. He probably would tell her some time later. It was only natural after all.

He hadn't taken his morning runs when he was with Diane. He'd run a few times after the incident with Graham, but had taken another route that didn't take him through the park. It wasn't fear as much as the unpleasant memory.

'Tomorrow I start again,' he told Leonie, 'back to my old run.' He thought it fitting that this was another sign of a return to the way things used to be.

He wasn't a believer in lightning striking twice in the same place, and Graham's attackers would be long gone. They would probably only have been there once, and the attack on Graham had been reported to the police. They would not return. Even if they did, they had no reason to target him. He could probably outrun them anyway if they decided to give chase.

He'd often wondered what he would do if he did see them again. Leonie hadn't been clear as to what she thought, only that he had fallen short, but Diane had tabled several options and they'd spoken about each. A lot depended on what the men were doing to their victim.

'A new beginning, darling,' he told Leonie the following morning, hugging her at the front door in his running outfit. His old run had assumed that status for both of them.

She held him, wanting to prolong the hug. 'Don't push too hard,' she said, and smiled.

He was feeling buoyant as he set out. A return to the way it had been. And should be. The sky was already a pale blue, deepening in colour, and Sandy, the grinning Labrador from the corner house, ran beside him for several blocks, her tongue moving backwards and forward like the windscreen wipers on a car, leaving him to chase a cocker spaniel as he finished the kilometre climb.

He entered Boronia Park. It felt good to be running as he always had, before…but that was now history. Things with Leonie had been restored. They were possibly better than they had been before. He passed the dead gum tree. Next marker was the grassy hollow.

Then he saw them. Two men were pushing a third man backwards and forwards between them. He was at least a hundred metres away, and couldn't tell if it was a game, or something more threatening. He could hardly believe it. Only the last time he'd run here the same thing had happened. Perhaps lightning did strike twice.

The gap closed quickly between them as he ran. Two things became clear. The two aggressors were not the same two as before, and what was happening was not a game.

He and Diane had discussed so many things he could have done when Graham was attacked. They'd looked at the pros and cons of each.

But none of them entered his thoughts. His mind was blank. He did know that he had to do something. But what?

He was fifty metres away. The three men were standing. One slapped the victim's face, an older man, and pushed him to the second man, who stood a couple of metres away. That man did the same and pushed him back. Their voices were raised, and the abused man, better dressed than his attackers, was pleading with them to stop.

The victim was thrown to the ground, but thankfully the two men didn't kick him. They continued the verbal barrage and stood, grinding their boots on his hands and chest instead. He tried to get up, but was pushed down again and threatened. Phillip could see the muddy boot imprints on the man's shirt, and the torn-away buttons.

For an instant, the early images returned, scar-face's smirking 'do you want some too' look, the brutality of the kicking, and the look of non-comprehension on Graham's face.

The men saw him coming. They stopped the verbal abuse, but one man kept his foot on the victim's chest to keep him on the ground. They weren't chastened by Phillip's appearance, and obviously had no intention of stopping what they were doing.

'Bugger off,' one said.

'Get lost,' from the other. 'It's nothing to do with you.'

Phillip doesn't move. He is not stilled by fear. Just determined. And they make no move towards him. 'I'll go,' he says, recalling later that he must have sounded ridiculously urbane, 'when this man,' and he points to the man on the ground, 'comes with me.'

'Do you want your face punched in?' the more aggressive of the two men snarled, moving towards him.

'If that's what it takes,' Phillip replies, raising his hands in a boxing pose, battling to keep his nerve, and for the first time knowing that he will not walk away. Not this time. He knows it now. He didn't know it before. And he readies himself for the attack, realising that a beating is the likely outcome. So be it.

'Come on, Kurt,' the less aggressive man said. 'We've had our fun.'

'Well, I haven't had mine yet,' the other said. 'I think we should teach this one a bloody good lesson,' but he hesitated in approaching Phillip.

'Let it go,' his companion said, and while Kurt seemed reluctant to do so, he still pushed his fist against Phillip's face, the bony knuckles pushing into his cheek, and snarled, 'It's your lucky day,' before both men swaggered away without a thought for the man on the ground.

Phillip could still feel the hardness of Kurt's knuckles as he helped the man to rise, and was thanked profusely. The man swore that he wasn't hurt, except for a bruised ego and the need for a new shirt. He shook Phillip's hand and, asking if there is anything he could do in return, walked gingerly towards the town.

*

Leonie is delighted by the change in Phillip after his run. He'd seemed more relaxed when he'd returned from his time away with Diane, but now he was really in high spirits. Something must have happened on the run. Perhaps the satisfaction of getting back to normal.

He greets Toby with a high five, and hugs her as she ladles out the porridge. 'A century next weekend,' he says to Toby when his son leaves for school. If there ever was a load on his shoulders, it's certainly been lifted now.

They have a few minutes before they have to leave to their respective schools, and Phillip is anxious to tell her what happened on his run.

'Two of them, roughing up the third, pushing him around, then throwing him on the ground and not letting him get up.'

'Uncanny,' Leonie replies. 'It happened again?'

'Lightning does strike twice,' he answers, keen to resume his story.

'Go on then. What happened?' Leonie asks. She's wary of asking him what he did, though she can tell from his mood that this time there must have been a satisfactory result.

'I confronted them. Said I wasn't going anywhere without the man on the ground.'

'Good for you.' She looks pleased. 'And then?'

'I must have looked menacing,' he tells Leonie. 'They probably thought I could do some real damage,' and feeling exalted, 'and I reckon I could have.'

'So you stood up to them,' she says with pride.

'Yes, I did. And I'm sure they would have gone on with it if I hadn't.'

'I'm proud of you.'

'Perhaps that's what I should have done before.'

'Perhaps not,' she answers. 'I was a little tough on you before. Every situation is different. I'm really sorry.'

'Tonight, Josephine,' he winks. 'Perhaps it's about time we had the Lathams and Hunts for dinner.'

He leaves for school whistling, doing a little comical skip in his gait for Leonie's benefit as he walks to the car.

*

Phillip doesn't know that Leonie, after months of searching, found only yesterday an original edition of *Bleak House*, the Dickens novel he'd been searching for and was unable to find. It was in an old second-hand bookshop, and she's had the book gift wrapped to present to him that very night.

He doesn't know that when she had been to the city the weekend before to meet old school friends, when he was at Diane's, she had also gone to the exclusive lingerie shop in the Queen Victoria Building, and purchased some very sexy black silk lingerie with pink ribbons that she plans to slip into after the special meal of beef bourguignon she'll prepare for that night when she arrives home from her teaching duties. She'll brush out her hair and let it fall below her shoulders. Stand before him.

And he certainly doesn't know of her meeting to thank Tim and two other teachers, all three of them colleagues from her school, and how they roared with laughter, recounting and ribbing each other about how good their acting performances were in Boronia Park that morning.

Thomas Carew

The misfortune of solitary and timid people – who are timid from self-consciousness – is just that, though they have eyes and open them wide, they see nothing or see everything in a false light, as though through coloured spectacles.

Ivan Turgenev, Diary of a Superfluous Man

1

'Come on, Thomas. You can dance with your Auntie Flo.'

I was grabbed by the arm and hauled on to the floor of the large downstairs room where my parents held their rare social gatherings. Everyone was dancing. It was a special occasion.

But that made no difference to me. Special occasion or not. I'd never danced. That's what grown-ups did. I was mortified. People might see me and laugh. I tried to protest, to pull away, but Auntie Flo would have none of it. She stood facing me, took one hand and held it upright. Then she took my other hand and, holding me closer than I wanted to be held, put my arm around her waist. I could feel the clammy and melting softness of it.

She began by taking a step backwards. But I wasn't ready, and I didn't know what to do anyway. I toppled forward and she had to rescue me before I fell on the floor.

Ten. Nine. Eight.

'Don't worry, Thomas. You'll learn,' she said, and we continued to rock backwards and forwards without going anywhere. The room was a blur of shifting colour. 'I'll show you later.'

I didn't tell her I didn't want to learn. Everyone had got up to dance, but they must have seen how clumsy I was. I imagined them talking about it later.

Seven. Six. Five. Four.

Most couples had now stopped, and were counting down with the voice on the radio. They were animated, their eyes alight, expectant. But Auntie Flo held on, and that made me more conspicuous.

Three. Two. One.

And then there was loud cheering. New Year 1952. Several people had squawker blowouts that added to the noise with their squealing. Others were hugging and saying things excitedly to each other. An older cousin was locked in an embrace, kissing his girlfriend. A few balloons were bobbing about above us, getting the occasional slap to send them on their way.

I felt Auntie Flo's large bosom against me, and the kiss. All breath and spittle. I wanted to crawl away and hide. And suddenly she was gone. People were moving around kissing each other. Pecks on cheeks.

Two other aunts came to kiss me.

'Why don't you kiss Mary Halloran, Tommy?' one of them said. 'She'd like that.'

Mary was the only other young child there.

I must have gone red, or crimson, or beetroot, but was rescued in time by my mother.

'Happy New Year, Tommy,' she said, and kissed me.

That was all right. I didn't mind that. 'It's very late for a four-year-old to still be up, but you've seen the new year in. There'll be a lot more to come. Time now for bed.'

I couldn't wait to dash upstairs.

My name's Thomas Carew, though everyone except Aunt Flo calls me Tommy. 'Why give a child a name,' she used to say, 'and not use it?' That was one of my earliest memories, and apart from those involving my mother and father, most are associated with Aunt Flo. I believe that's short for Florence.

At lunch the next day, I didn't wake up in time for breakfast. My mother and father were talking about her. Adults mistakenly assume that very young children 'don't take anything in', that it's beyond them. I understood it all. If you'll excuse the poetic licence, it went something like this.

'Flo comes on a bit strong, doesn't she?'

'She's always had very strong views about most things, dear.'

'And doesn't mind forcing them on everyone prepared to listen.'

'And even those not prepared to listen.'

'I was referring to last night. Not so much what she said, but how she behaved. "Larger than life". Isn't that what young people say now.'

'I think so. That, or over the top.'

'Yes, over the top. It embarrasses me. I hope it didn't upset others.'

'I don't think so. Everyone knows Flo. Even our friends. They all know what to expect.'

'I suppose so. If only she could behave more…well, if only she could be more normal.'

'But what's normal? That is Flo's normal.'

I remember my father looking at me then. I'd stopped eating my cornflakes, my spoon stilled, and he could probably see my curiosity. Nothing was said about Flo after that.

I understand now what they meant. Auntie Flo was jolly and loud, her buxom frame lending weight to the opinions she freely expressed as universal truths. She'd only have been in her thirties at the time, but even then, her hair was greying and her face becoming plethoric. She was my mother's sister, and the differences between them couldn't have been more marked.

She was good to me. At least, she was well-meaning. She had never married, and I think I was regarded as more than just a nephew.

As for what my mother said all those years ago about her being over the top, I'm sure she was right. I remember her not so long ago at the funeral of a family friend, in a long sweeping dress of chiffon, high heels and with her hair tied back tightly across her scalp to fully expose her made-up face. Hardly funeral garb.

My parents met in a youth group in Homebush, and were married in the war years when my father was on leave. 1942. They lived for a couple of years with my grandparents in North Strathfield, and moved into a large home in Denistone when I was one. They were planning for a bigger family but I was to be the only one.

By today's standards, my mother and father would be called prim and proper. They were not averse to having fun, but there were appropriate limits, as their talk about Flo illustrated. How many times in my growing years did I hear that word, appropriate. 'That wasn't appropriate behaviour.' 'Is that an appropriate thing to say?'

My father was tall and slender with dark hair and a slight limp from the war years. He was a religious man if it's possible to be religious without being a regular churchgoer. I always thought his work in the tax office was appropriate for someone who thought people should be accountable at all times. I had to be, but I could never accuse him of being unfair.

My mother was a gentle soul who shared his views, possibly more from association than original conviction. She was more demonstrative than him, though mothers usually are. She had done a secretary's course after leaving school, and resumed work as a temp after I began school. Petite, with dark hair and a pale face, she was very attentive to me. I was always her baby.

While I'm recalling these early years, I should mention Thelma, my father's sister, a stout, red-faced and often breathless woman. She'd sometimes be called on to mind me after infants' school when my mother had her temp work. I found her bossy. I was allowed a glass of milk and one biscuit. No more. I was required to sit and talk to her before being released to go upstairs and do my homework, whether I had any or not.

'Don't slouch, Tommy,' she'd say. Slouching must have been a cardinal sin. 'Sit up straight, and don't fidget when I'm talking to you.'

It was little wonder I was pleased when my mother got home.

'Was it all right?' she'd ask, conscious I think of what Thelma was like.

'Yes, Mum,' I'd answer.

Looking back, I think Thelma's need to quell my unseemly behaviour was on a spectrum with a need to create stability in a chaotic world, including her own marriage to Ivan, a gruff and difficult man.

It mightn't therefore be surprising that their son Warren was always in trouble. He was my own age and went to the same school, but we didn't play together, and when Aunt Thelma came to mind me, Warren was left with their neighbours next door. I'm not sure whose decision that was. The few times I saw him with Aunt Thelma, there seemed to be open hostility between them. Not the affection there was between me and my mother. He'd do everything he could to get her annoyed, and succeeded without even trying.

He had the same effect on his teachers, and was often called to the office to face the infants' mistress. He was sometimes in the office with the counsellor, and I can only imagine her futile attempts to set him on the right track.

His theft became open knowledge at the school, and therefore throughout the parent community. He'd stolen a teacher's purse, and had taken out the money before putting it back. I don't know how this was discovered, but it was. He would have denied it. I heard my parents speaking about it, probably with stronger words than appropriate.

'Poor Thelma.'

'Poor Thelma nothing! She could do more to keep him in check. Show a bit more affection rather than tying him down, making him bend to her ridiculous rules.'

'Perhaps it's not all her fault, or Ivan's. Don't you think some children are born different, some loving, some cooperative, some timid, some nasty.'

'No, I don't believe that. Anyway, I heard Ivan took the belt to him, really gave him a thrashing. He deserved it.'

'You don't believe that, and neither do I.'

'No, I suppose not.'

I shuddered when I heard this. I had never been spanked. But I wasn't sorry. I didn't like him. He was a boaster and a teaser. 'Shy boy. Shy boy,' he'd call out to me in the playground. And as the years passed, the names became less flattering. Scaredy-cat. Weakling. Coward.

That must have been the beginning. Growing up, we don't really know if the demons we have are shared. We are torn between believing that we are all the same, and that something is peculiar to us alone. Probably more the latter. It was the first time I remember being called shy. And the first time it had been thrown at me as an accusation.

It was to be the first of many.

2

The years of growing up were happy for me. At home, I was showered with affection, particularly by my mother. There's a consensus that single children are usually overindulged, spoilt. You might be waiting for me to refute that but I'm inclined to agree.

I always had my own room, and in the late primary school years, my father bought me a grand-looking desk. It may have been second-hand, but it was better than the tiny school-sized desk I had. It was big with a leather inset top, and three drawers on each side of where I put my feet. He was a good handyman and built bookshelves and drawers where I could store everything I needed for school. He gave me some of his books, the ones I prized, and I dutifully covered them in plastic before shelving them.

Our school holidays, always in early January, were at either Forster or Kiama, and were anxiously awaited in the years before I became a teenager and was seduced by other interests. I can see my mother shaking her head now, and commiserating with my father about how she'd lost her baby boy.

I enjoyed school, and was so anxious not to displease, I was a favourite with the teachers, and popular with my peers. There were challenges for me, though, that might not have bothered other children.

I was a good reader. I learned to read early, and the teachers praised me for using the right expression. We were reading a play called *Henry the Monster* in fourth class and discussing what it was about. I know now why Miss Hambley chose it. It presented the message that we all have fears. We all fear rejection, and we all have self-doubts, even the bullies in the play.

Henry is a new student at his school and is bullied because he's blue, furry and very tall. He makes a lot of new friends, but he's also the target of bullies.

Miss Hambley announced that our class would perform the play on the school's upcoming play night. 'We need a narrator, a Henry, a bully called Garth,' and she listed the characters, male and female. 'Tommy, you'd be the perfect narrator.'

I was stricken. I could sit at my front desk and read with expression, particularly when all the children had their heads down following the script, but I couldn't make all those appearances, walking on and off the stage in front of the whole school, and all the parents. I couldn't do it. But I couldn't say no to Miss Hambley in front of the class.

She could see my fear and spoke to me after school. 'You're our best reader, Tommy, but I could tell you were frightened. Don't you want to do it?'

'I don't think I can, miss. Not in front of all those people. I'll freeze. I don't want to disappoint you, miss, but…' I didn't have to continue.

'Do you remember what the play is about, Tommy?' she said gently.

'Bullying.'

'Yes, but more than that. It's about the fears we have. I have them. I'll tell you a big secret, Tommy, because I know you won't tell anyone. I'm afraid of the dark.'

I'd never felt closer to a teacher, but she continued, 'You're afraid of, well, I'm not sure, perhaps looking foolish, people judging you, doing the wrong thing. I'd really like you to be the narrator. We won't say any more about it now, though. We'll talk again tomorrow.'

We did talk again and Miss Hambley had thought of what she hoped might be a solution. I could be the narrator, but not appear on stage. I would be in the wings with a microphone. No one would see me. They'd only hear me. I was still scared, but I wanted to please Miss Hambley. She'd been so understanding.

And that's what happened. The play was a great success. It was a challenge for me, but I managed. Some of you will be incredulous, believing taking a major role in a play is no big deal, that it's a privilege most children would fight to get. I think it made me realise for the first time that my fear was a cross I had to bear.

There were a few more incidents like that in my school career. In the early years of high school, we'd been studying *The Merchant of Venice*, and the English master thought it would be a good idea to perform it in front of the school. A cast was selected and, without consultation, I was chosen to be Antonio. I should have been pleased with that because I was chosen to portray a kind and generous nobleman, but the thought of acting the part led to a great deal of anguish and several sleepless nights. I kept thinking of Antonio bearing his chest with a flourish as Shylock waited with his knife to take his pound of flesh. Can you imagine the reaction of a hall full of adolescents?

Fortunately, the priority of other events in the school calendar prevented the play from going ahead, and saved me from the sickness that was likely to strike at the most inopportune of times.

Please don't think I was a sissy. I was good at sport, and joined in all the games with the other students, as long as I wasn't singled out for special attention. A couple of times in both primary and high school, I was asked to be a leader of a sports team. Some teachers chose the boys who were particularly good in the sport we were playing. Others tried to give every student a turn, and that made it hard to avoid.

There was usually little responsibility in being appointed, though I found it very challenging when you were made leader of one of two or three teams, and the leaders had to take it in turns to select students one at a time. I still find that practice odious. The same students were always chosen last.

When I was in sixth class, there was a sports afternoon for all of sixth grade. There were four different rotations, including hurdling, throwing heavy medicine balls, and using the shot put and javelin. It was closely supervised. I had been told that I was to take charge of taking the equipment back to the sports shed, and had been given the keys. It was a big responsibility. Other students would help.

But they didn't. I don't think the teachers nominated helpers. Several students were still there as I began to collect the hurdles. Two boys said they would collect their school bags from the classroom and return to help. They didn't. No one else offered to help. They simply walked away. I'm not suggesting they were mean. They might have assumed that someone had taken care of it.

You'll be saying to yourself, 'Why didn't you ask?' I couldn't. Was it because it was expecting too much? Was it because in some strange way I was drawing attention to myself? Was it because attention-getting was implied superiority? How many times over the years do you think I've asked myself those questions?

It took me an hour and a half to get all the equipment to the sports shed by myself, and of course I missed the bus and had a long walk home to a highly anxious mother and Auntie Flo.

It didn't stop there. What happened must have been observed by a teacher or parent. I never found out who, but the following day there was an assembly for all of the sixth classes, and the principal tore strips off the boys, saying how thoughtless they'd been. He praised me and condemned them for their lack of consideration. They all looked in my direction. I wished I'd been invisible. The attention was far worse than the attention I tried so hard to avoid in doing the work.

I don't believe it was any coincidence that the next day I was asked to visit the school counsellor. She was an older woman with a lined face, though the lines were not those of stress or anger and added a wisdom and gentleness. She came and sat next to me rather than sit behind a desk. I didn't see much purpose in our talk then, but I have more of an appreciation of it now. Of course I can't repeat it exactly so you'll have to be content with this version.

'That was an impressive thing you did with the sporting equipment, Tommy. Carrying it all by yourself.'

'Thanks, miss.'

'Did you do it to save the other boys?'

'Yes, I suppose I did.'

'Did you ever think of asking them to help?'

'I did, but… I didn't want…to inconvenience them.'

'But it must have been a big inconvenience for you?'

'Yes, miss.'

'Did you think at the time that some of the boys might have been willing to help, if they'd been asked?'

'I think it was expecting too much. They may not have liked it.'

'Tell me, Tommy, what do you think you'd like to do when you leave school?'

'I don't know.'

'Do you think it might be something with people, something working with your hands, something with numbers or documents…'

This took place on a Friday, and the weekend couldn't come fast enough. Luckily, I wasn't left to stew in my room the whole time, licking my wounds. We went to a drive-in at Dundas. Technology has done away with them now, but they were all the rage then. My father went for ice cream, and I had the back seat to myself, and a clear line of vision between my mother and father.

I had never been so moved by anything as I was that night. Remember, I was closing in on adolescence. The film was Rodger's and Hammerstein's *Carousel*. I'm glad my parents couldn't see my wet face when the lead characters sang 'If I loved you…'

Boys weren't supposed to be sentimental. I was, but it would be a long time before I'd admit it. I knew I'd feel for someone the way the singers felt about each other, but would anyone ever feel that way about me?

*

The idea of star-crossed lovers finding each other across a crowded room is melodrama. Yet in that crowded room, I believe you might be aware of a presence, whether it's a manner, or how something is said rather than what. It's as if something flows from one person to another. The romantic in me hopes it flows both ways, but I'm not so sure.

That is how it was with Susan. At a fundraiser for local teenagers, the speaker had finished and I was making my way to the refreshment table at the back of the hall when we bumped into each other. Probably brushed against rather than bumped.

'I'm so sorry,' I said, turning to see her for the first time.

'No, I should be sorry,' she said quietly. 'I wasn't watching where I was going.'

'I'm sure I was the one at fault,' I answered.

She looked at me curiously with the palest of blue eyes beneath a mop of strawberry-blonde hair. Neither of us ventured to say the obvious, that it was no one's fault, that it was nothing at all, almost inevitable in a crowded room.

'I'm Susan,' she said looking self-conscious.

I'm Tommy,' I felt able to reply, not wanting to be too presumptuous.

We must have said a few things after that. I can't remember what they were, but we were only together for a minute before a group of her friends came and spirited her away. I think she looked back, but I might be mistaken.

Susan Bright. I've already given a brief description, but left out that she was slim and pretty. We were the same age, lived in the same suburb, but had gone to different schools. Like me, she was an only child with caring parents. She was studying architecture at university.

I thought about her that night in my room, my sanctuary. I liked her. Felt drawn to her. But there'd already been numerous contacts with girls like it. You dwell on them, possibly even fantasise about them, and, soon after, the memory is lost, spirited away like she had been.

3

I met Susan again three weeks later. It was another meeting of the charity we both supported as volunteers. The organisation had by now assigned roles to the volunteers, one of which was kitchen duty after the meetings. Susan and I were assigned the same duty that day. Fate operates in mysterious ways.

There were four of us, and the other two left, leaving Susan sitting at the table with me. She made no move to go. Neither did I. We began to talk. I only remember parts of what she said. I have filled in the rest, but believe it is true to the spirit of our conversation.

We started with pleasantries.

'I'm glad you're here, Tommy,' she began, and blushed.

'And I'm pleased you are too,' I replied and, because I feared an awkward silence, 'You did a great job in there.' I pointed to the kitchen.

I noticed she wasn't moved by the compliment. 'I imagine you joined for the same reason as me, to help teenagers.'

'I'm not much beyond one myself, so I think I can relate to some of their concerns.'

'Particularly when things aren't all they should be at home.'

'I think you'd be very sensitive to the problems that they have, that all people have.' I wondered if expecting an answer was asking her to reveal too much.

'Why do you say that, Tommy?'

I was a little embarrassed because it was a question that called for my opinion of her, but I was buoyed by how the conversation was flowing. 'I sometimes feel so much for people, it hurts. And when you looked at me at that first meeting we had, I thought you might feel the same.'

'I do.' She blushed again and this time she looked pleased. 'I know what you mean about feeling so much about people, and the sad thing is there's not a lot we can do about it.'

'At least we're doing something now, even if it is only a drop in the ocean.' I felt an overwhelming need to ask her what she thought of me at that first meeting, but I didn't. What could she say? She'd feel obliged to say something flattering to stroke my ego. And that's probably what I wanted.

We continued by sharing details of our personal lives. Our parents, our lack of siblings, our schooling, our interests. It struck me later that we shared this information without asking many questions, and I wondered if we both thought to do so might be seen as prying.

I think we were both enjoying ourselves. I know I was. And if she wasn't, she could easily have excused herself. The next part of our conversation was more revealing. I think our vulnerabilities had fallen away. We were comfortable together.

'Tommy, I think you've seen by now that I'm really very shy. And I hope you're not offended, but I think you are too. You don't have to answer.'

'I want to answer, Susan. I don't think I've met anyone as shy as I am. And yes, I know you are too. It was another thing I felt at that first meeting when we were apologising to each other.'

'You felt it, at a glance?'

'Yes.' She nodded. 'I have those feelings about people too.'

I remember her smiling, and knew that a story would follow.

'If you think you're shy, listen to this.' She was relaxed, and her excitement was infectious. 'I went to St Kevin's, a Catholic school, and we always put on a concert for the parents at the end of the year, something Christmassy. I was in fourth class and we had to sing "Give Me Joy in My Heart". Several of the better singers were chosen to sing a stanza as a solo. I was one of them. I told the teacher I couldn't face it, but she insisted. Said it was what I needed to bring me out of myself. Those were her very words.'

'I can't wait for the rest,' I said. Already it was similar to my fourth-class experience.

'You probably know the song. It's a favourite in the schools. I had to sing,

> Give me joy in my heart, keep me serving
> Give me love in my heart, I pray
> Give me love in my heart, keep me serving
> Keep me serving till the end of day

I was petrified. There was a sea of faces all watching me. Got to the second line and ran off the stage.'

I surprised myself by laughing. I didn't want to hurt her feelings, not knowing if the trauma remained. But she began laughing too, so I asked what happened.

'Sister Bernadette stopped playing the piano. There was a buzz around the audience, concern, I think, but I ran out the stage door. My parents came looking and found me in the playground.'

'It's uncanny, Susan,' I began when we'd stopped laughing, 'but I had an almost identical experience in fourth class. Our class had to per-form the play *Henry the Monster* in front of the school and parents, and I was chosen to be the narrator. Like you, I told the teacher I couldn't stand on the stage in front of all those people.'

'You didn't walk off like me?'

'Not quite. I was still the narrator, but I did my narrating from the wings, invisible to the audience and using a microphone. There was one good thing about it.'

'What's that?' She was smiling broadly.

'I didn't have to learn my lines. Just read it all.'

Is love the capacity to share your vulnerability? It must be part of it. I'd found a kindred spirit. I'd never been able to face my shyness so openly, not even with my mother. I wanted to tell Susan that. I wanted to hold her. I wanted to know if she felt the same. She was looking at me fondly, and all these years later I don't think she'd have minded.

It was getting dark then, and we said our goodbyes. I didn't want her to go, and once outside the hall, she lingered as if she was waiting for me to say something.

'I hope I see you soon,' she said.

'I hope so too,' I answered. Something more needed to be said, but I left it at that.

I was miserable for the next few days. I wondered what she was doing. Surely it couldn't have been that hard to give her a call. But it was and, for the first time, I wondered if there was something wrong with me, something that went far beyond the scope of shyness.

Another three weeks passed before I saw her again at one of the meetings. She seemed pleased to see me, but was more subdued. She was battling to recapture the openness we'd achieved the last time we'd met.

'I wondered how you were,' she said, her eyes lowered.

I knew what her question left unsaid. 'I thought about you a lot,' I replied, thinking it necessary to take things further.

'Did you?' There may have been a hint of surprise.

We were silent for half a minute. Some teens were speaking loudly beside us, one of them talking about having seen the musical *Oliver*, showing in Sydney at that time.

I saw Susan look at me for a fraction of a second and look away. I knew what she was thinking.

We had different responsibilities that day and didn't see each other until it was time to leave. I was feeling wretched. I'm not sure, but I think she might have been too.

'I'll see you next week, Susan,' I said, trying at the same time to hide my misery and be propitiatory.

It was some comfort that I only had a week to wait. The charity had been organising a picnic day for the young teens in a local park. There were to be a variety of activities, prizes, and a lunch. It was to be staffed by the volunteers. For me, the day couldn't come soon enough.

I'd been wondering how I might find Susan after our last meeting, but my anxiety was short-lived. She waved from a distance, and I waved back. I could see her smile. She was carrying large containers of food, and I was lugging trestles for the tables. There was a small army of helpers.

Throughout the morning, we worked side by side, supervising the activities, even joining in. It gave me a feeling of our togetherness, of a common purpose. I think she felt it too. We chatted and laughed a lot. It was another side of the openness we'd shared swapping stories about our shyness. It was giving me a fuller and more glowing picture of the girl who was starting to mean the world to me.

We joined the queue circling around the tables for lunch, and when we weren't helping ourselves, we served each other, she spooning tabouli and ham on my plate while I forked slaw and chicken onto hers. We sat together to eat on seats scattered in pairs or small clusters, shoulders touching. Young love, you might say. First love anyway.

She took our empty plates to the table, and was returning when a man appeared beside her, circling her waist with his arm, and kissing her on the cheek. 'Hello, darling,' he said, 'surprise, surprise.'

Susan smiled lamely and seemed embarrassed. She looked to me anxiously, then turned to her companion, and back to me. Left, right, left, a dangerous road to cross. I was paralysed.

'Andrew.' The man reached out his hand to me by way of introduction.

'This is Tommy, Andrew,' Susan said hurriedly before I could respond. She must have been determined to do what was natural and polite, and to arrest her own embarrassment.

I acknowledged Andrew as courteously as I could, and hurried away, using sickness as an excuse to avoid the cleaning up responsibilities. I'd never feigned sickness before, and haven't since. I went straight to my room, and didn't come out for dinner that night. My mother was worried but thought it best to let things rest.

Andrew Spiteri, tall, Italian ancestry, and with all the trappings of assured good looks, was five years older than Susan. He was dressed in tailored caramel-coloured slacks, while we were in jeans. Andrew had used his skills as a real estate agent to purchase property, and to be comfortably well off. I have no reason to think that the transactions weren't above board. I'm sure he was decent enough.

I'd been a fool. I wasn't duped. Susan hadn't promised anything. She hadn't lied or mislead me. Andrew had more to offer in just about every way. I could understand why she might find him attractive.

I could say I might have appeared to be a bear with a sore head for the next few days, but I don't think I did. I fought the pain and tried to show more kindness and consideration than usual. It was noticed. The pain wasn't. The next charity meeting was three weeks away. I'd decided to withdraw anyway. I liked the work and thought I was contributing, but didn't think I could handle being there with Susan.

When my mother knocked on my door the following night to say there was someone to see me, I never even considered Susan. After the problems with shyness we'd spoken about, it must have nearly torn her apart to come.

She looked forlorn standing in the family room. She'd introduced herself to my parents, but I entered on an awkward silence and she looked at me helplessly. As I led her upstairs, her eyes red and swollen, my parents gave each other a knowing look and watched our climb.

Once inside my room, Susan began to tremble, and I held her, feeling a moment's pleasure in my own circle of pain, a satisfaction that I'd been able to act in a way the world would call normal.

We stood like that for a couple of minutes, not saying a word. I didn't want to let go. I don't think she did either. She was still clinging to me as she began talking.

'Tommy, I know I hurt you terribly. I'll never forgive myself.'

There are times to keep quiet. This was one. I thought of telling her there was nothing to forgive, but I was enjoying holding her, and I knew she had a story to tell.

'He asked me to marry him.'

That was another blow. Could things get any worse? She must have felt its impact as my hold slackened, and she let go of me to search for tissues in her bag. My dawning hope that this might be a chance at reconciliation had been snatched away.

She understood my reaction. 'Tommy, I said I wasn't ready. I couldn't commit.'

To my mind, that was only half a solution. She hadn't refused. Readiness usually becomes reality when the time is right. I was still silent, waiting to see why I was in the picture, if I was at all. Was she here to soothe my wounds or to offer a solution? I'm sorry if that sounds too harsh. It was only a fleeting thought. She was hurting and my heart went out to her. I felt like weeping with her. For her.

'He asked me about you. I told him you were special, and he wanted to know why.'

'What did you tell him?' It was time to speak.

'I said we were very much alike, and he wanted to know how. I was stumped for a few seconds, and then I remembered our funny stories about shyness. So I said you were shy like me.'

'I got the impression he isn't the slightest bit shy.'

'He's not.'

'So what did he say?'

'He asked me if I thought being shy was being too proud to make a fool of yourself. I said there might be some truth in that, but then he took it further and asked me if shy people might be egotists because they're too concerned about what people think of them.'

'What did you say to all that?'

'I wasn't going to argue with him. I don't think he was spoiling for a fight. But I did say you were the least egotistical person I know.'

We were quiet for a while. It must have been hard for the girl who ran off the stage at the school concert to come knocking on my door, and she had been more open about her feelings for me, if you could read between the lines. But I still wasn't sure where it left me.

I've usually found that after a very revealing show of emotion, a person's defences very quickly spring into action, and they return to their normal persona. So it was with Susan. She apologised again for hurting me, and said she didn't want anything to come between us. She wanted nothing to change.

I wanted to ask where I fitted into the picture with Andrew, or where he fitted into the picture with me. But I wasn't going to press. We'd come far enough in one night. I knew I'd go to bed later thinking of her saying she wanted nothing to change for us. Things can't remain the same indefinitely, but I suppose that had been encouragement enough.

She gave me a brief hug before she left. Nothing was said about further contact. I walked her downstairs, past the inquisitive eyes of my mother, and saw her to her car in the darkness.

4

At the next meeting of the charity, Susan was a little more reserved than normal. I had expected it, but had been looking forward to the meeting, hoping that I would learn more, not so much about her feelings for Andrew, but about her feelings for me.

'Hello, Tommy.' Her greeting was warm. She must have been a little embarrassed, but determined to be her normal self. As we were called to our seats to listen to the speaker, she apologised again, not for what had happened on the picnic day, but for arriving at my home without warning, and for making a scene.

'I was delighted to see you,' I said, 'and you didn't make a scene. I know how hard that must have been for you.'

'I think it was the hardest thing I've ever done. Your parents must have seen I'd been crying. Whatever did they think? Some hysterical female pursuing their son.'

'They didn't think that at all,' I answered as we were sitting down.

Not that I knew what they thought. They never asked me about Susan, probably believing that if I needed to talk, I would. My mother must have assumed that the love life of her newly adult son was out of bounds. But Susan was obviously feeling ashamed, not that she should have been, and I needed to say something to reassure her.

It was the first time we'd sat together at one of the meetings, and I had to fight the temptation of looking at her, and allowing my hand to creep towards hers.

We stayed behind after the meeting, not because we'd planned to do so, because we both assumed we would. I wondered if her comment that she wanted nothing to change was the end of the matter, or the beginning of something more. And I didn't know which I'd choose.

She wanted to say more, because she ushered me outside, and we sat in her car.

'I haven't accepted his proposal, Tommy,' she began. The use of my name softened the message. 'I didn't even do the usual thing and say I needed time to think about it.'

I had the feeling that she might have been distancing herself from Andrew for my benefit. 'Has he asked you again?' I asked hoarsely.

'No, said he's giving me breathing space, but he will.'

The next step was mine. The obvious question was 'What will you say when he asks you?' But I couldn't ask it, and I don't think it was my dreaded shyness. I didn't want to know. Or feared knowing.

The other plain question that's asked when someone is facing Susan's dilemma, is 'Do you love him?' A 'yes' answer usually eliminates any uncertainty. I thought to ask that was presuming too much, so I couched my question as a statement. 'I suppose if you love someone…' The rest was left hanging in the air.

'Yes,' Susan answered. 'Love is everything.'

She wasn't being evasive. She simply hadn't answered in the way I'd expected. I was still unsure about her feelings for Andrew.

'He has a lot to offer. More than I could give you,' I said, hoping that didn't sound self-deprecating. I suppose I was being provocative, wanting her to talk about love and where it belonged for her.

'Tommy,' she said, 'we don't always love the person who's got everything.'

That was promising. I felt rebuked, but it was worth it.

'And I wouldn't like you to think that I'd be seduced by money or good looks.'

'I've never thought that, Susan.' I answered, feeling upbeat.

'Love's not like that,' she continued, determined to hammer home the point. 'It's not what we have. It's who we are.'

Bravo, I thought, and she could read my approval.

'I'll just climb down from the soapbox.' She'd seen my reaction and smiled.

*

We did go and see *Oliver*. I didn't ask. Neither did she. Another couple organising a theatre party had two tickets to spare when others pulled out, and asked us together. It wasn't difficult to accept.

We were both a captive audience. Andrew was forgotten and we were together holding hands. We sensed the excitement in each other, sitting in the richly upholstered maroon seats and looking down on the brightly coloured stage.

And when Oliver, sang 'Where is Love', we both squeezed each other's hands. I think she would have leant closer if it hadn't been for the armrest between us.

We were quiet on the way home. Words were superfluous.

*

It was a long time before we saw each other again. The charity had cancelled a regular meeting owing to the sickness of committee members.

She was reserved when we did meet. It could have been light from the sun slanting through the window, but she seemed to be flushed. 'Hello. Tommy,' she said, polite enough, but not with much warmth.

'It's so good to see you,' I answered, feeling like I was treading on eggshells. 'It's been such a long time.'

Susan was unusually direct. Our time apart must have been playing on her mind. 'I came to see you, made a fool of myself in front of your parents…and you. I thought you might at least… She left the rest hanging in the air like an accusation.

I didn't say anything, but stood there awkwardly, hands in my pockets. I thought of saying I didn't contact her because she might be busy with Andrew, but that wouldn't have been fair. Or honest.

'Tommy,' she sighed, 'what am I going to do with you?' It was the sort of comment a loving mother makes to her impish son.

She softened towards me after that, but we didn't get any further chance to talk. I was living a roller-coaster of highs and lows. Meeting every three weeks with all the constraints that involved was hardly

162

enough, and I knew she felt it. Unless I did something, it would be another three weeks.

*

At the next meeting, Susan was more distant. We didn't have the opportunity to speak before the meeting, but she had given me a half wave. She was on cleaning-up duty in the kitchen and I resolved to wait for her to finish. I couldn't wait to see her.

'Tommy.'

I heard my name. I turned. It wasn't Susan. It was Andrew.

'It is Tommy, isn't it?' He'd obviously come to see Susan. He sat down beside me to wait for her.

I knew my plans were thwarted, my happiness checked.

'So this is where it all happens,' he said.

I wasn't sure if he meant 'all' between Susan and me, or 'all' with the charity, but I answered, 'Yes.'

'She thinks the world of you, you know.'

My heart lifted. 'And I do of her,' I said.

'She believes you have a lot in common.'

'Yes, I think we do,' I answered. 'We're like soulmates,' I nearly said, but didn't.

'She knows what it's like to be shy,' Andrew smiled. 'We've had some funny times together trying to make her more confident.'

'Yes,' I replied, it's one of the many things we have in common.' I must have been trying to score points.

'She said you were even more shy than she is. That's hard to believe. Anyway, she's really sorry for you.'

Susan had finished her duty and joined us, this time with no embarrassment. She seemed neither particularly pleased nor disappointed at seeing Andrew.

The half minute of conversation that followed was forced. The three of us spoke of the charity and what it was achieving. I could see Andrew signalling to Susan. Time to go.

'Bye, Tommy,' she said, and left with him.

For weeks, I'd try to re-imagine the tone of her voice, the emotion behind the look. Was there any meaning a desperate mind could salvage from the literal 'Bye, Tommy'? Nothing very positive, I decided.

But that was the least of my worries. Andrew hadn't been trying to hurt, but his comment that Susan was really sorry for me, cut like a knife. Was this my lure for Susan, that she was sorry for me, that I needed protection from an indifferent world? Did her sympathy come from the recognition that she suffered from the same affliction I did? Where did love enter this? Did it at all?

*

Strange, but I'd never seen her handwriting, but I knew the letter was from her from the sticker on the envelope. Pleasure and fear were in balance as I opened it. It was brief and to the point.

Dear Tommy,

I know there is no chance of seeing you before the next meeting, but thought it necessary to tell you before then. I have accepted Andrew's proposal. I hope you'll be happy for me. I look forward to seeing you at the next meeting. Perhaps we can talk then.

Love, Susan.

I don't have to tell you my reaction. I cried, sitting perfectly still on the bed in my room with the letter in my lap, and remaining that way for an hour after the tears had stopped. I was annoyed at first, thinking she might have told me before she accepted, but I knew she wasn't answerable to me. Her behaviour had been beyond reproach.

This is the time a person who's lost in love revisits the past to make sense of things, to find rhyme or reason. Your mind latches onto a word, a look, a time together that might call into question the wisdom of a decision that has torn you apart, that makes you consider the possibility of appeal. So it was for me.

'Perhaps we can talk,' she'd written. On the one hand, I wanted to know why. And why only perhaps? On the other hand, I felt there was no need. She didn't have to explain. No reasons were necessary.

We did meet, sitting on a park bench near the meeting hall. I was uncertain how I would find her, but she was more loving than I could remember, except for the time at *Oliver*.

I'd decided to let her do the talking. I wasn't going to behave like the little boy who's lost his favourite toy. And I wasn't going to ask why. Things could never be that simple. She could tell I was upset, and in some strange way, I think she was too. I remember wondering if her tears were those of sympathy for me, or for her own loss.

She told me Andrew had claimed her for his own. What sort of word was that?

Claimed. Is that what you do with people? Claim them? Wasn't it more to do than submitting a form? And what was her part in it all? Did being claimed give no right of refusal?

We were silent for a long while. I didn't ask her about the wedding, or future meetings at the charity, or even if I'd ever see her again. I did wish her well. She must have seen my struggle to do so.

She held me before she left. We stood in the park clinging to each other, as women pushed their strollers, children kicked footballs and workers hurried home, just for once not caring if we made a spectacle of ourselves.

5

Susan wasn't at the next meeting, but that was no surprise. Of course I did the usual soul searching. Was it because she would be uncomfortable facing me, or was it because she was too busy with wedding preparations. I didn't like either reason.

The wedding invitation was a surprise. I suppose I'd been used to most people having longer engagements. It was so sudden, and must have been orchestrated by Andrew. I'd also nursed a hope that Susan might reconsider, and had been living in limbo since our talk in the park. Engagements are often broken when partners understand what's at stake. But the invitation, decorated with blue doves and bordered in gold, gave our last conversation an awful reality.

I was grateful for being invited alone, and imagined the debate between Susan and Andrew as to whether I should be invited at all, or with a partner. But Susan understood, and I'm sure she wanted me there.

Most of you have probably experienced what I went through in those three months before the wedding. The opiate of suffering, the depression, the self-doubt. The latter was the worst. I kept thinking of how she held me when we'd last met, and wondered if things could have been any different.

Shortly after the invitation arrived, my mother knocked quietly on my door, asked tentatively if she could come in, and joined me sitting on the bed. 'Tommy, that girl who came some time ago, she was important to you, wasn't she?'

'Yes, Mum,' I answered. Children often deny their parents the knowledge that they're hurting, pretending they don't need protection, but I saw no reason to deny it.

'And she was the one who sent the wedding invitation?'

'Yes. Her name's Susan.'

'I seem to remember her saying that,' my mother replied. 'Tommy, I'm so sorry,' and she put her arm around my shoulders. She didn't ask what my intentions had been, and I suppose it was obvious I hadn't been myself.

I mention this because it shows how we can be too hasty to judge. We all think we have left our parents behind in worldly wisdom. This ultra-conservative, staid woman did understand, and had been worried about me, biding her time to speak.

*

There've been a few significant days in my life, like the beginning of my final year exams, my eighteenth birthday, and the charity picnic. Susan's wedding was another. Because the day is special, you look for some sign of it in the natural world to ratify its significance.

I stood at my window looking at the pastel blue sky with skimming threads of cloud, wondering what Susan was doing now, what she was thinking, wondering if she was giving me a thought.

A formal wedding meant tuxedo. I couldn't imagine anything else for Andrew. I drove to the church in the tuxedo I'd hired with no expectations. Susan would have no time for me. Better that, I thought, than a 'hello, thanks for coming' from the happy couple as they moved down the line with their limited ration of thanks.

I introduced myself to her parents in the church grounds before we entered the church. They seemed to know my name. 'How is she?' I asked. The more I thought about it later, the more I thought it was a foolish question. I hope it didn't offend.

Her father looked at me with a curious smile, before he joined other well-wishers, but her mother seemed to understand, and took me by the arm. 'We've heard so much about you, Tommy,' she said.

I know the stock response is 'All good, I hope,' but I avoided that. 'I imagine she's really excited,' I said instead, hoping to make amends for having been too direct.

'Malcolm thinks Andrew's wonderful,' she said, pursuing her own thoughts rather than answering the question.

'Don't you, Mrs Bright?' I replied.

'Yes, yes, of course.' She was suddenly defensive. 'When Susan started to talk about you, I thought, well, I thought…excuse me, Tommy.' Her husband was calling for her. There were a dozen others she had to greet.

What did she think? If only she'd had time to finish. I entered the church and sat in an aisle seat towards the front. Susan would pass close by as she entered on the arm of her father.

The church had a high vaulted ceiling supported by massive wooden beams. Beyond the altar, the back of the church was a blaze of brilliantly coloured stained glass, and side windows showed Mary and the baby Jesus trapped in stained glass and swirls of lead. They seemed to bathe the interior in a warm light. A golden eagle fronted the pulpit.

An organ was playing religious music. I allowed my mind to wander. There was comfort here. For a few minutes, my concerns seemed very small. The world was so much bigger. I hadn't noticed the church filling.

There was a buzz of movement and voices. People were looking around at the entrance, craning to see. Andrew and his best man were standing at the front near the altar in grey tuxedos. We all stood as Pachelbel's Canon flowed from the organ, and the bridesmaid dressed in apricot preceded Susan, who held her father's arm.

Of course I wondered how she'd cope. I knew this was one performance she wouldn't flee from. She was looking straight ahead, not turning to mouth a 'hello' to people on either side of the aisle, not looking ahead at Andrew, who'd turned to admire her. I could see the effort it took, and wondered if she'd noticed me as she passed. Felt my presence perhaps.

I didn't really follow the service. I was watching her, even though I couldn't see her face. And I couldn't really see the shape of her figure, standing perfectly still, because it was hidden by her train. But I stored the image in my mind for later retrieval. While Andrew's vows were loud and clear, Susan's were barely audible.

*

At the reception, I was placed next to Tash, or Natasha, an extroverted friend of Susan's, who obviously knew a lot about me. She was tall, leggy with an open face that went pink with the slightest exertion. After the meal, she stood, placed a hand on my shoulder, and said, 'You are going to dance with me, Tommy Carew.'

The dance floor was packed, so I was grateful that we could do little more than shuffle on the spot, invisible to prying eyes. She was restrained in her dancing, though I sensed that the very opposite was her true style. She seemed to understand.

'Susan told me a lot about you, Tommy, about how shy you were,' she said when we sat down.

'And I don't know anything about you, Tash,' I answered.

'It'll keep,' she laughed. 'When she told me you were shy, I thought you were a perfect match for her.'

'You don't now?' I said, not to be provocative. I was interested in what she had to say.

'No, of course not. That's when Andrew came along. Better still, I thought. He can bring her out of herself.' Tash mustn't have known anything about my feelings for Susan.

But her perspective on things didn't concern me. Her view was different from that of Susan's mother. We all see things differently. We all draw on different data.

We listened to the speeches. The best man worked unsuccessfully at trying to be funny. Andrew was assured, peddling the usual clichés about being the luckiest man in the world. Susan smiled. Occasionally laughed. And the dancing resumed.

I was watching the couples pressed together on the dance floor when I felt another tap on the shoulder. I turned. It was Susan.

'Dance with me, Tommy,' she said. There was an urgency about her voice. She led me to the dance floor, and held me, close but not touching.

'Are you cold?' I asked. I realised later what an odd question it was.

I think I must have sensed a trembling. It might have been me and not her.

She shook her head.

'You look wonderful, Susan.'

She seemed emotional. I'm not saying I was the cause. A wedding has to be emotionally charged. There was a lightness in our touch. I held her as though she were fragile, not wanting to crush her dress, or crush something within her. Something so pure and beautiful required a gentleness, a feather touch. Don't ask me how, but I know she felt the same.

'Are you all right, Tommy?' she asked, looking concerned.

It was almost too much to bear. On such an occasion, her occasion, why ask a question like that? I battled for the right words.

'Yes, I'm fine,' I answered, but I don't think I fooled her.

She let go of me slowly, squeezed my hand, avoiding my eyes, and left.

*

We keep saying things are final. That they're all over. But how many finalities are there? Her acceptance of Andrew's proposal was final. The actual wedding and exchange of vows was final. But her goodbye to her guests was for me the most final of all. It was now a fait accompli.

There were no individual goodbyes. The newlyweds ran the gauntlet, being showered with confetti, and drove away in Andrew's Porsche.

The celebration was over. The mood had changed. It was like a party's sad deflated balloon. People began to gather their belongings and head for home.

Tash had wound down. The key to wind her up had gone missing. Mrs Bright made a point of finding me to say goodbye. I felt I had an ally there.

I stood where I was and watched the car turn a corner out of sight. Out of my life. I felt a great emptiness as though a great chunk of my identity had been torn away, leaving me the near impossible task of reinventing myself.

6

There were highs and lows for me over the next eighteen months. I sometimes wondered if my healing skin of glossy pink was becoming a calloused hide as one dream eclipsed another. New buds insensibly spring up but, looking back, I believe Susan was always there in my thoughts. And memory has a sensitive trigger, a song, a look, a laugh, the same coloured hair or blouse.

I didn't sit at home and mope. I usually went out in a group, the one involved with the charity. Of course, pairings usually spring up in groups and so it was for me, but nothing serious.

Amber was a red-haired dynamo with what to me was an unusually zestful thirst for life. She didn't oppose our sharing a quiet evening at home watching a movie, but I think for her it was a novel idea. I always thought she was manic in her need to grasp life by the throat.

She knew I was shy, but taking the lead in virtually everything was not something that troubled her. I'm still not sure whether I was a challenge, the woman who can change the man for the better, whether I had some real appeal as her complete opposite, or whether feeling can emerge between the most unlikely people in the most unusual circumstances. I incline to the latter. When she found herself a go-getting man who shared her need to massage life to her needs, and milk its pleasures, I was relieved.

Megan was an attractive brown-eyed girl with waist-length mid-brown hair, who made me question the notion of type when it came to shyness. I know Susan's shyness was different from mine, but Megan's was different again. She compensated for it by drawing attention to herself, using her sexiness as a drawcard. People would initiate contact with her, and save her from starting any conversation. When she did engage others in talk, she was unsure of herself and poor with conversation. Shyness? You might think it isn't, particularly if you saw how Megan flaunted herself, wearing short skirts that exposed the full length of her shapely legs, and smoked through a cigarette holder, leaning her head back and blowing smoke rings into the air. You'd think that was conceit, or the behaviour of an extrovert.

I admit to being attracted to Megan. I sensed her shyness. Mine was obvious to her. We were close to each other in the group for six weeks, until her attention-seeking behaviour began to annoy me. I've always found that is the beginning of the end. Even the smallest quirk like a facial expression can start to irritate and becomes a cancer. By then, I knew only too well that the road towards the emerald city might be paved by broken stone.

It was fortunate for me that she moved interstate with her work. For me to have to explain seeing less of her was a challenge I would have found hard to face.

*

Her letter surprised. I hadn't heard anything from her, or about her since her wedding day eighteen months ago. It was a typed letter that read,

> Dear Tommy,
> I will be at the park, on the same park seat we sat on once before, on Saturday 12th at 2 p.m. I will understand if, for whatever reason, you can't be there.
> Love, Susan.

You can imagine how I mulled over the semantics of that letter. 'If for whatever reason' could mean because I'd found someone else, because I'd made other plans, or simply because I didn't want to see her any more. And it was signed 'love'. Some people do that with just about any correspondence, but knowing Susan as I thought I did, I saw it as significant.

I felt excited until I realised she might simply have wanted to pass on information. Perhaps she wanted to explain a few things that were left unexplained, perhaps they were going to live overseas. Perhaps she was pregnant. But I did want to see her.

I paced up and down in my room for an hour before I had to leave. I suppose I didn't want my enthusiasm to be too obvious. Even then, I left early, entered the park from the far entrance and took my time admiring the flowers.

I'd played out several scenarios in my mind as to how I'd greet her. A cheery long-time-no-see, a warm really-good-to-see-you-Susan, or a slightly open-armed approach hoping she might also open her arms for a hug. Uncertain as to why she wanted to meet, I decided I'd take my lead from her.

I left my pretend flower-watching at two minutes before two p.m. and walked towards the seat. And there she was, coming towards me from the other direction. Pale blue blouse. Bone-coloured slacks. Hair bobbing neatly around her shoulders. Walking at a measured pace. The same figure. Her face might have been thinner. Excuse another cliché, but she took my breath away.

'Really good to see you, Tommy.' She'd already stolen my thunder. 'Let's sit down.'

I said something earlier about new buds insensibly springing up. Well, they were nipped in the bud as I sat next to Susan and felt the warmth of her arm against mine.

'Have you been all right, Tommy?' she began as we were sitting, looking at my face as though to read it. 'Have you been happy?'

'Yes, I'm fine, Susan,' I said, and hoped it didn't sound too abrupt. I could hardly say I'd been deliriously happy when she'd left with Andrew.

'And your shyness, Tommy, is it…the same?' I think she avoided asking if it were better.

'I suppose it's the same, Susan,' I answered, uncertain why this was the start of our conversation. 'I suppose the only time I lost some of the shyness when I was…when we…' It was an admission I hadn't planned to make, but it was the truth.

'Oh, Tommy,' she turned urgently towards me, 'is that really true?' She seemed surprised. So was I.

'You must know I was at my talkative best when we had our talks.' I'd gone this far. I might as well go further. 'Don't you remember?'

'Every word,' she said softly, lowering her eyes.

We were silent for a minute after that, but it wasn't a void. Feeling was hovering there.

'And you, Susan, is your shyness the same?' I might have started as she did, and asked if she were happy, but that might have been too pointed.

'The same for me,' she answered. 'Andrew did everything he could to make me overcome my shyness. Once, he called upon me without warning, introduced me as one of the speakers at a public meeting. Only needed to talk for a few minutes. I couldn't. I just couldn't. He apologised later.'

I was tempted to say that was cruel, but I didn't. His intentions were probably noble.

'I said the same,' she continued, 'but while I might have made some gains, I think with the best of intentions, Andrew might have made me worse. When someone expects you to do something, forces you to do it, you clam up even more.'

Was this a sign of some tension between them? The thought died quickly. Every relationship has small misunderstandings. And this was one. I'd already accepted that this was a catch-up meeting and nothing more, and I was grateful for it.

We were like two old flames, recapturing some of our fond history, sharing memories that were ours alone. And it was all very proper, sitting together on the park bench.

'Look at those birds,' I enthused. 'Are they parakeets, or lorikeets? I never did know the difference.'

Some brightly coloured birds swooped together from tree to tree in front of us. Why did I say that? I think I felt some tension creeping in, but I did want to know more about how things were with Andrew. I didn't have to wait long.

'We've decided to separate, Tommy.'

A few moments of silence and, shocked, I turned to look intently at Susan. She was looking down, biting her lip, but our hands did search for each other's at the same time.

Why, was the automatic reaction, but I wasn't going to ask. This was what she'd come to tell me. Besides, how could anyone answer that question in a way that's intelligible to someone else? Some failed marriages may be the result of a single cause, like violence, child abuse or other criminal activity, but for most, the reasons are many and varied, and usually so complex, they are even beyond the understanding of those involved.

'I'm so sorry, Susan,' I whispered, and squeezed her hand.

It was as if her answer echoed my thoughts. 'I can't explain why,' she said. 'It's never simple is it, Tommy?' She wasn't here to give a litany of excuses. 'I will say this, though. He wasn't unkind. It's just that sometimes I felt…like I didn't know him.'

It's strange how that simple answer meant so much to me. I suppose it was because, whatever the shortcomings in our relationship, I did feel we knew each other.

'So what will you do now?' I asked.

'I'm going away.'

'For good?' I asked, already feeling that having re-entered my life, even for only a few minutes, I didn't want her to leave it as precipitately.

'I don't know. I'm moving away from here to live, at least for a while, probably somewhere on the south coast.'

'By yourself?'

'I think so, unless I meet someone who wants to share.' She was looking down, scuffing the grass with her shoe.

'But won't it be lonely?' I persisted.

'Probably not as lonely as my marriage was,' she answered.

'I don't like to think of you in some strange place, all by yourself.'

'I might not be lonely. Someone might be interested.' She still had her eyes lowered.

After a minute's silence that seemed to last forever, she straightened, smoothed her slacks across her knees, and stood. 'I just wanted you to know,' she said.

I stood, and we did hold each other, reaching out at the same time, grasping. We held each other as if there was no tomorrow.

'I won't be going for a week or two,' she said softly. 'Bye, Tommy.'

I watched her go.

Owen Barlow

I had else been perfect,
Whole as the marble, founded as the rock,
As broad and general as the casing air,
But now I am cabin'd, cribb'd, confined, bound in
To saucy doubts and fears.
William Shakespeare, Macbeth, Act III, sc. 4

1

You can tell when a class of students, whatever their age, is engaged. The students listen attentively. Make eye contact with the teacher. Sometimes some of them nod in agreement and lean forward in expectation, or the need to contribute. When not engaged, the polite students usually pay the courtesy of feigned listening, though their minds are elsewhere, and can only be resuscitated to academic consciousness by a question from the teacher that jolts them from their lethargy.

Owen's classes were always engaged. He was a fine lecturer, popular with the students, spending a lot of time preparing, and planning motivational beginnings for his classes, believing it important to snatch student interest from the outset, and not let it go.

He lectured in the Faculty of Education at Macquarie University, and his students, predominantly young women, were training to be primary school teachers. The program involved some mass lectures of a hundred and twenty students, the whole year's cohort, but most classes were tutorials of thirty or so students that developed the subject matter introduced in the mass lectures.

'Last week, I said I'd give you all a Smartie, boys and girls, if you worked hard in class.' Owen has already started the lesson, but is mimicking an infant's teacher. After the chorus of voices asking for their much-deserved Smartie, he asks, 'That's an example of what?'

It takes the class a few seconds to catch on, recalling the recent lecture, before a few call out, 'Positive reinforcement.'

'Someone define it for me,' he asks.

'Saying something positive to increase a response, like giving a Smartie for hard work,' one of the more extroverted young women answers. 'I've worked really hard, Owen.'

The class laughs. She is not being rude. Owen encourages a certain amount of fun, and first names are not frowned upon by some lecturers at tertiary level.

'You'll get your Smartie, Michelle,' he retorts. 'It's obvious that school students need a lot of positive reinforcement. You had many examples of that in the lecture, but can anyone suggest why it might not be a good thing all the time?'

The class is stumped. That wasn't mentioned in the lecture. There are a few seconds of silence until one of the mature-age students suggests, 'Might children learn to use it to their advantage? Might it stop them from learning what they really need to learn to improve?'

'Ten Smarties for you, Joan,' and there is a chorus of appreciative clapping. 'Now what about negative reinforcement? Anyone?'

'Reinforcing the way bad behaviour is dealt with,' a young man answers.

'Would anyone like to challenge that?' Owen asks, and several hands are raised.

The answer isn't correct but he doesn't want to tell the student he's wrong in front of the class. He could make light of it by saying there are no Smarties for him, but he knows how fragile egos can be.

The tutorial continues in this way for another twenty minutes, questioning the understanding of given information, and introducing new material. He gives the class a few quick exercises.

'A Smartie for you, Owen,' Michelle says as the class leaves the room. She's smiling. 'That was a really good lesson.'

'Thanks for the…' and Owen pauses.

'Positive reinforcement,' they say together, and laugh.

*

Owen was always going to be a teacher if his childhood pursuits had anything to do with it. As a boy, he preferred playing schools to superheroes. His first playmate, the boy next door, told Owen it wasn't much fun being the student all the time, and stopped playing with him. His sisters were a couple of years older, and he couldn't teach them much. And when they agreed to play, they also wanted their turn as the teacher. So Owen often taught an imaginary class, chalk at the ready, asking questions aloud to named students. 'Why is that, Amy? Can you give me an example of that, Stephen?' nodding or shaking his head.

His desire to teach remained with him, and he later trained to be a high school teacher, and was fortunate to be appointed to a local secondary school as a teacher of English and history.

His father was proud of Owen for following in his footsteps, having been a teacher his whole working life. 'Never missed a day,' was a frequent boast he made when he thought the younger generation was guilty of being too lax. He was disappointed, though, when Owen left the school for the university, even though he did so to teach teachers in training. His father still believed he had abandoned ship.

His mother was proud of him too, not because of any academic achievement, but because he had grown into a considerate and god-fearing young man, who had married an equally kind girl who had given him a lovely daughter. Family was everything after all.

Christened Owen Percy Barlow, the Percy after his mother's father, he was a gentle boy, doted on by his mother, coddled by one sister and ignored by the other. He attended the local state primary and high schools where he was well-liked by the teachers and his peers. He represented the school district in athletics, and was made a prefect. Unlike many adolescents, he didn't have anything to prove to others, and being handsome was an asset in a co-educational high school.

He attended the local church throughout adolescence, but stopped going in his late teens, not from any disillusionment, but because he believed it didn't provide the answers he sought that could only be found in the less dogmatic teachings of the outside world. Yet he'd always argue it was an important foundation.

*

Saturday at last. He loved his job but the weekends were special. Never a dull moment but peaceful nonetheless. Owen always returned from his morning run to a house buzzing with activity.

'Owen, can you take Cassie to her yoga?' Kate asks, climbing into her tracksuit bottoms.

'Ten minutes, Daddy dear,' Cassie, finishing toast and coffee, blows him a kiss.

'And could you stop at Darrell Lea and get chocolates for the Manuals? You haven't forgotten dinner tonight, have you?'

'Yes, yes, and no,' Owen replies, after processing the questions in good humour. 'How is Cassie getting home?'

'Damian's parents are bringing her back at five,' Kate answers. 'I'll take the Datsun,' she continues, heading for the door with her tennis racquet. 'And when I'm gone, don't go talking to any strange women.'

'But all women are strange,' he quips.

She hurries back to kiss him, tousles his hair and hurries out.

Kate Sharpe shared with Owen an early conviction of what she wanted to be. Instead of schools, she played hospitals or doctors and nurses. She'd laugh with Owen, telling him of how her neighbourhood friends were called upon as patients to be lovingly tended by her nursing skills.

'Childhood games couldn't have been much fun for them,' Owen ribs her, 'lying flat on their backs.'

She'd been a good student, represented her school in tennis, studied a degree in nursing at the University of Technology, Sydney, and worked in the maternity ward at the local hospital. Owen would often tease her, saying he needed a good dose of tender, loving care. She'd either provide it, or call him a little baby.

They met when Kate took her niece to a fete at Owen's school. Owen had organised a stall where people paid for balls to knock down skittles. If they managed to knock all the skittles down with the three balls, they won a cuddly toy donated by a local manufacturer of toys. Kate did.

'You win a cuddly toy,' Owen called, handing her a lifelike koala, and replacing the skittles.

'Does it cuddle me?' Kate asked, pretending to be serious.

'No, you cuddle it,' Owen answered, smiling.

'So I don't get a cuddle,' Kate pouted, only realising later how provocative that sounded, thinking he would be wary of such a forward young woman. He wasn't.

That was the beginning of their relationship. They were married shortly afterwards.

*

They knew something was wrong when Cassie returned home. Her eyes were red and swollen, and she hurried straight to her room without saying a word. Owen and Kate exchanged concerned looks.

'Damian,' Kate said. 'I'll go,' and she followed Cassie upstairs.

At fifteen, Cassie was the joy of their lives. Already with the figure of a grown woman, she didn't yet enjoy the maturity of one. And unlike most of her peers, she wasn't afraid to admit it. That combination usually raises concerns for parents, and Kate and Owen were no different. But while many of their friends complained about the turbulent behaviour of their teenage daughters, they were silently thankful. Cassie was no trouble at all.

Owen had to wait till later that night as they undressed for bed to hear why Cassie had been upset. He was anxious about it throughout their evening dinner date with the Manuals.

'Same old story,' Kate began.

'I was afraid of that,' Owen replied. He didn't have to be told the story's name or its plot.

'They were having a kiss and a cuddle when Damian tried for more,' Kate explains.

'What!' Owen was instantly alarmed.

'Don't worry,' she calmed him. 'Cassie didn't let him.'

'Well, what…' Owen began.

'Just a bit free and easy with his hands, we don't need details, and he put his tongue in her mouth.'

'And Cassie?' Owen was alarmed. He was well aware of the path that lay ahead for his daughter, but was determined she should walk it when she was ready.

Kate managed a smile. 'Gross, Cassie kept saying over and over,' Kate reported, 'and yuk.'

'I suppose there'll be more nights like this,' Owen said, turning out the light.

2

'You all know I love dogs,' he began his Monday mass lecture to the second-year students. He paused and there were a few surprised looks. 'Well, I've invented the Callisthenic Canine Cavorting Contraption Containing Covert Curriculum Considerations, and he displayed an overhead of a dog-exercising machine that had a sequence of exercises the dog must follow once it enters the chute of the machine. Appreciative applause and grins followed.

'The covert curriculum considerations are these. When you develop a plan for learning for students, whether for two weeks or six years, there are four steps to follow, just as there are four exercises the dog has to complete in order. They are outcomes or objectives, content or subject matter, methods or teaching strategies, and assessment or evaluation. Remember O-C-M-E. They have been called the curriculum commonplaces.'

Owen continues his lecture, making frequent reference to the dog exercising machine as he explains the four steps, and, once finished, bowing to the applause, retreats to the staffroom for his morning tea.

'Go well?' Shirley, the special education lecturer asks.

'Yes, they're a great group,' Owen answers.

'And they respond to good teaching,' she compliments him. He is known as one of the better and more popular lecturers. 'By the way, Lynne came in earlier. Wants to see you. Said it was important.'

Lynne is the dean, and Owen decides to go straight away, though he has no idea for what. It might have something to do with the research grant application he's heading.

*

Lynne greeted him warmly and motioned him to a chair, coming from her desk to sit opposite him. She comes straight to the point. 'Owen, I've received a complaint. It's in writing, so I have to follow it up.'

Owen was startled. It must be about him, or why else would he have been summoned?

Lynne could see his surprise, and hurried to explain. 'Natalie Clements. Final year mature age student. There has to be some explanation for this. Some sort of misunderstanding perhaps?'

What happened the last time he spoke to Natalie started to become clearer. Why she had complained didn't. He gave a resigned shrug. Better to learn the limits of his offence, if that's what it was. How it had been constructed and reconstructed by Natalie. What another's memory had done with the creep of feeling from each imagined revisiting.

There'd been a complaint, but was it reported as some petty and forgivable lapse, a grievance that could be dismissed with a smiling, there, that's been dealt with, or was it to be hauled from a misguided innocence to a serious personal affront? To be waved with the banner of persecution. Proclaimed as an example of the dragon-slayer seeking justice from the oppressor.

'Well, is it true, Owen? She said you kissed her.'

'Yes, I suppose I did.'

'You suppose. Surely you either did or didn't. I'll take that as a yes.'

Owen remained silent, head down, already looking beaten. Or was it possibly growing guilt or contrition. His integrity had never been questioned before. Whatever, it halted the dean's emerging irritation. She was a few years younger than Owen, with cropped, mousy-coloured hair, and power-dressed in dark stockings and black skirt for eagerly anticipated promotion. But they'd always enjoyed a good professional relationship.

'You'd better tell me what happened, Owen,' she said more gently. 'Please understand, it may be just a storm in a teacup, but I have to ask. My hands are tied.'

At least he was still Owen. Not stripped of identity, to suffer the anonymity of the miscreant. That, Owen reckoned, showed some confederacy.

'I don't know what to say,' he said quietly, deep in thought. 'I kissed her. We'd been discussing the assignment. She hadn't understood what was being asked. It was the one on reinforcement. She was battling to understand that negative reinforcement…'

'Owen, I don't need to know what your assignment was about.' There was no impatience in her interruption. She wanted this complaint to be settled speedily with a minimum of fuss, and not be a long, drawn-out issue with repercussions beyond the faculty. 'Just tell me what happened.'

'I don't remember how it all changed. It was reinforcement one minute, and her marriage the next,' Owen finally began to explain. 'She must have brought it up. I wouldn't have asked. At first she was curious, bright even. Then she became sombre.'

He paused, recalling how forlorn she had looked, sitting cross-legged in her ragged denim jeans and white sloppy joe, urgency in her violet eyes, her long, dark hair gathered to the front over one shoulder and hanging halfway to her waist, watching him intently as she spoke.

'For a long while,' he continued, 'she'd suspected there was something between her husband and his secretary. She was always mentioned in their conversations, he danced with her a bit too intimately at the office party, she found notes and receipts for gifts, smears on his shirts that might have been face powder, rouge, that sort of thing. Then work demands increased, when they never had before, and he had to stay back. Would come home late, one night didn't come home at all, seemed to have lost interest in her. She said something to me, rather delicately, but enough to lead me to believe that sex between them rarely happened, and when it did, it was far from tender, even rough, a frustrated longing of his that she wasn't able to satisfy, or a punishment.'

'And that's when you kissed her.' The dean leant forward, a gesture of sorts, like meeting him half way, reading the resignation in his lowered eyes.

He nodded. How much more did the dean need to know? The why of it all hardly mattered. Judgements were based on actions. Sometimes simply giving an action a name was enough to damn the perpetrator. And how could he articulate the why anyway? It was an impulse, a rare moment of connection, a gesture of tenderness and empathy. He'd leant forward as she'd looked up, and the kiss lightly brushed her lips. She'd looked startled, but only for a moment.

At the time, he thought she seemed pleased. Or at least more at ease. After all, she'd revealed the most intimate details of her life. She had touched his arm before the kiss, or was that his imagination? His kiss was a statement, however clumsy, that he was in tune with her feelings. If only he'd known it would be so unwelcome.

'Owen,' the dean began, 'I'm sorry I have to ask, but there are different sorts of kisses. I'm not a voyeur, but can you tell me…' She left the rest unsaid.

How do you dissect a kiss? Surely they're not all the same. This was a kiss that came from feeling, gentle and sweet, a fleeting touch that leaves a taste of tenderness and intimacy. It wasn't the more vigorous kiss where couples search for meaning or try to find themselves in each other's mouths. And it certainly wasn't the kiss offered in lust. God forbid that he might be tarred with the brush of the abuser.

'I get it, Owen,' the dean commented after a lengthy silence, when Owen hadn't answered. 'I can imagine what sort of kiss it was. I'm sorry. I shouldn't have asked. I think I understand now. I'm really sorry about this,' and she reached out as though she were going to place a consoling hand on his shoulder, but thought better of it, and left her hand in the air, making it a gesture.

'The thought that you were trying to, you know…' she half-smiled, 'is ridiculous. You'd have to agree, though, in retrospect,' she felt the need to counsel, and to state what officialdom decreed, 'it wasn't discreet. Perhaps you should have changed the subject when she started to talk about her marriage. That was probably asking for trouble. What's more, you can never be certain how something like that is seen by others. A man of, what is it, forty-two, forty-three, kissing a much younger female student, is not a good look, however innocent or caring the motive, particularly in this day and age.'

Owen watched the dean. Watched her lips moving, even saw the concern in her eyes, the faint brush of down on her upper lip. For half a minute, he didn't hear the words. He felt he was dissociated, looking on at the miming of someone else's unfolding scenario. Not grasping how the situation applied to him. Am I remorseful, he asked himself. Should I be? What am I really feeling?

'I really can understand what you're feeling, Owen. Please know that. You'll have to apologise, though,' he suddenly heard the dean say. He knew it was protocol, and that Lynne saw it that way, that she would have avoided it if she could, but it still made him feel culpable. 'Something low key,' she said, feeling sorry for him, leaving him to wonder what a low-key apology involved. 'I'm sure it will all go away with a minimum of fuss.'

*

'I kissed a girl on Tuesday. One of the students,' he told Kate that afternoon.

'Oh yes,' she answered light-heartedly, undisturbed as she added pasta to the boiling water, but turning around and seeing that Owen was looking uncomfortable, she left the saucepan to boil, rubbed her hands on her apron, and sat down beside him on the divan in the family room next to the kitchen.

'And what sort of kiss was it?' she quipped, trying to lighten his mood, but sensing there was more to the story he was about to tell. 'Was it like this?' and she gently pecked him on the cheek, her eyes alight with mischief. 'Or was it like this?' She pulled him down on the lounge and gave him a prolonged kiss on the mouth. 'I'll bet it wasn't like that,' she said playfully.

He could taste the pasta sauce she had tested for flavour and spooned into another saucepan.

189

'The student complained. Went to the dean. I was called to account today. Had to explain to Lynne.'

'They're not serious,' Kate protested, and could see Owen's uneasiness. She didn't have to be told what sort of kiss it was, or why it was given. 'You'd better tell me exactly what happened.' She was no longer playful.

Owen told her, his explanation fuller than the one he gave the dean. It was more an account of how he'd felt as the talk with the student about her failing marriage unfolded, how he'd felt sorry for her, how empathy had grown.

Kate had been privy to his innermost feelings for half a lifetime, and understood him when they both knew others might not. There were no secrets between them. 'So what happens now?' she asked, her concern transparent on a face pink and damp from her cooking. 'Did you convince Lynne it was nothing?'

'I think she knows that, but I have to apologise to the student.' He held up a hand to halt Kate's protest. 'I don't blame Lynne. I'm sure she was sympathetic, and would like it all to go away, but she has to follow official procedure.'

'Seems to me you're a sitting duck.' Kate was aggrieved for her husband. 'A student can say anything she likes…and you can't tell me it works both ways.'

'Pasta bolognese, yum!' Cassie, their teenage daughter, entered in a rush, dropping her school bag on the tiled kitchen floor, and bringing their talk to an abrupt end. 'My favourite.'

'Enter the whirlwind,' Kate said laughingly, suddenly brightening. 'You must have been able to smell it from, well, from wherever you've been.'

'Mum's pasta bol. I could smell it anywhere. And why is Daddy so quiet? Did I interrupt something?'

She approached him from behind, and threw her arms around his neck as he sat on the divan. Cassie was green-eyed, willowy and attractive. Nascent womanhood had been kind to her, opening a world of enticing possibilities that presently outweighed the other pitfalls of adolescence.

'Hard day at the office,' he answered jokingly, forcing good humour.

Kate and Cassie managed to keep up a continuous light-hearted dialogue throughout the meal. Kate spoke of accidents with bedpans at the hospital, and Cassie reported a student proving a teacher wrong. Owen tried his best to be his usual amiable self. Kate cast occasional concerned looks in his direction.

'You're in an unusually good mood,' he told Cassie, trying to be upbeat. 'No doubt it has something to do with Damian,' and he winked at Kate across the table.

'He apologised. I know Mum told you all about it.' Cassie was exuberant. 'He was really upset. I thought he was going to cry. He bought me chocolates,' and she tapped her schoolbag to show where they were. 'If you're a good boy, Daddy, I'll give you one later.'

'I'll try really hard,' Owen replied, as Cassie climbed the stairs to her room.

3

Natalie's marriage to Blair was failing, probably already beyond reclaim. Like almost everyone in her position, she'd grasp at an explanation till something more plausible occurred to her, and it would be grasped with equal conviction, while the other was let go. A spray of chaotic possibilities like a hose not held.

Was it something to do with how people behaved towards each other in the larger scheme of things? Natalie referred to class when she spoke to Owen, and apologised for being 'politically incorrect'. But for want of a better word, didn't class, call it socio-economic level, present a whole range of different sensibilities, differences in how people viewed education and the Arts, differences in recreation and how they spoke and entertained, differences in taste and how they interpreted what was socially polite and acceptable?

Blair came from a loving working-class family, Natalie from an upwardly mobile middle-class family. Different sensibilities perhaps, but enough to destroy a marriage?

Was it Natalie's need to better herself through tertiary education? Owen had heard of failed marriages among his mature-age students when husbands couldn't cope, not only because the wives weren't available as much to cater for their needs, that was the given excuse, but because the wives suddenly blossomed into more self-confident and independent people, no longer drudges tied to the family home and dependent on their husbands.

Blair had started work in a trade as soon as he left school. So apart from those considerations, might he have been resentful of what he erroneously assumed to be Natalie's presumed superiority?

Was it simply a matter of incompatibilities that couldn't be breached? No two people are exactly alike, but are there some differences that are insurmountable, where the theory that complementary personalities are good for a successful partnership, doesn't hold water? The female-mannered and refined lover of ballet, and the raucous pub-frequenting blokey man. The extrovert and the introvert. The adventurer and the stay-at-home.

Natalie was quiet, serious and introspective, whereas Blair was more immediate and hale-fellow-well-met.

If Owen had known all this, and he didn't, though he had intuited pieces of it, he would have said all three. It was apparent to him that they had begun the downward spiral from disappointment to disenchantment to resentment to anger, a spiral that sometimes ended with indifference.

When she'd started the washing one Saturday morning, Natalie noticed a red smear on the collar of Blair's shirt. When asked, Blair was dismissive, admitting it was a misdirected kiss from one of the women customers thanking him. It was obviously lipstick. Natalie was suspicious but didn't pursue the matter.

The following week, there was what could only have been face powder, and a thin line of what might have been mascara on his shirt. It looked as if some attempt had been made to swab it clean, but had only managed to spread it over a larger if paler area. She had ample reason to be concerned now, but when tackled about it, Blair brushed it aside with no attempt to deny it.

A few weeks later, he didn't return home, saying he was at a conference. Natalie asked what conference there was in his particular trade, and was ignored. Further questions were also ignored. Matters had come to a head.

'Just be open with me, Blair. You're having an affair, aren't you?' she asked as calmly as she could.

They were still at the dinner table. That was the only place she was sure to find him.

'Of course not!' he answered peremptorily, sounding hostile more than indignant, in the hope of silencing her.

'I only want the truth, Blair.' She raised her voice. 'You at least owe me that. The lipstick, blusher, mascara, the so-called conference.'

Blair felt cornered. 'If I was having an affair, you could hardly blame me,' he replied scornfully.

Natalie was furious. Cheating was bad enough, but to justify it by blaming her was inexcusable. 'I'll take that as a yes.' She was hostile now. 'And I'd like to hear why I might be to blame.'

'You're hardly the loving wife. Ever since you started that bloody course, things haven't been the same. You're never here, and when you are, you have your head in a book. You're not looking after yourself any more. Look at you! And you think you're so bloody high and mighty.'

'Even if there was a grain of truth in any of those things, and there's not, is that reason enough to start cheating? You ought to be proud of your wife for what she's trying to achieve, not trying to put her down at every opportunity.'

'I'd rather have a full-time wife, and not a…not a…

Natalie didn't wait for the rest. It wouldn't be complimentary. 'Who is she anyway? Or is there more than one? Yes, that'd be right.'

'Go to hell.' Blair stood suddenly, sending his chair crashing backwards to the floor.

'At least I didn't go off with another man, though I'm thinking now I should have. Perhaps I still will.'

'And who'd want you?' He had the knives out now, intent on hurting her.

Natalie was seeing red. 'Plenty of men! Not everyone sees me the way you do.'

'Is that right! Some of your fancy friends at the university?'

'Yes, lots of them.' She wanted to return hurt with hurt now. 'Even one of the lecturers likes me.'

'What the hell does that mean?' The possibility of a likely threat aroused Blair. 'Tell me! Tell me!' he ordered, approaching her menacingly.

She held her ground and said nothing.

Catching the eight seventeen bus to the university where he was employed as a teacher educator was a ritual. Why take a car when parking costs were so exorbitant, when there was a bus stop only a hundred metres from his home, and when it stopped at the university gates?

Apart from those making an occasional trip, some of the passengers had their own rituals, and had come to know each other.

Frank was a gently spoken senior with silvery hair who visited the hospital every day to see his chronically ill wife. He always carried a Tupperware container of biscuits he'd baked the night before.

Mrs Luscombe (she didn't like being called Daphne), older still with patchy blue-grey hair, was a stout woman with a large stomach, and a mole on the side of her nose. She travelled three days each week to help her daughter with the children.

Elizabeth, an attractive thirty-year-old mother was always dressed immaculately in silk blouse and black skirt. She worked as a secretary, and carried her half-heels in a bag, so she could slip out of her walking shoes and enter the office looking elegant.

There were also several university students who were familiar by sight but not by name. They usually managed a cheerful hello or wave.

The day after his talk with the dean was bleak. The sky was a louring dark, and the bus was late, but just in time for him to escape the mist of rain. Not a good omen for those like Owen who thought the weather might have some portent for the day.

'More last night on this Greg Daikin thing,' Elizabeth ventured after initial hellos. 'I'm so disappointed. Such a lovely man in the interviews I've seen. I thought he was one of the better ministers. I liked him. I feel really let down. Do you think it's true?' she asked no one in particular.

A few days earlier, the television news had presented a catalogue of complaints about Daikin's alleged sexual innuendo, his exposing himself to a woman, and his very inappropriate touching. The initial allegation had caused an avalanche of formerly timid women who followed the whistle blower. Safety in numbers. Pictures of three female victims, two of them parliamentarians, were shown. One was obviously distressed as she recounted her experience. Daikin was seen protesting his innocence and claiming that he would fight the charges and seek justice against those who'd made them.

'Well, of course it's true,' Daphne responded through the pursed lips of conviction and rectitude. 'Surely you don't believe what you see on those television interviews. Butter wouldn't melt in their mouths, but take them away from the cameras…' She was obviously on a hobby horse, and one that excused her belittling of anyone who dared challenge her. 'They should all be castrated.'

'Who's they?' two of the university students chorused. 'Do you mean every male politician, or all men in general?' one of them continued, lightly mocking, intent to prick the inflated balloon of Daphne's bigotry. 'Castration's a bit severe, isn't it? I mean cut off his balls? He didn't rape anyone.'

Daphne was annoyed, offended by the crudity of the university students, and of being interrupted in mid-flight. She was used to a captive audience and rarely challenged. 'They're all the same,' she mumbled.

'Thanks a lot,' one of the male students said softly, smiling at his friend, and winking at Owen.

'You'd have to agree, Daphne,' Frank said quietly, always seeking accord, 'we have some very capable politicians who really want to make a difference, make the country a better place. Look at what Bayliss did for the flood victims, and what Bishop's doing with the UN.'

All was quiet for a few moments. Perhaps Daphne thought the others were ganging up on her.

'What do you think, Owen?' Frank asked.

'I agree, Frank,' Owen replied with no real passion. 'You can't tar everyone with the same brush.'

'Well, you've heard my opinion,' Daphne said after a short silence, as if that were sufficient defence, and she buried her head in a dog-eared paperback with obvious ill humour.

Elizabeth smiled at Owen and shrugged as if to confirm the futility of reasoned argument. He nodded and turned to look out the window at the thickening grey.

*

Owen sat alone in the television room watching the late-night news. The lead item concerned a junior political staffer who was sexually assaulted some weeks before in Parliament House. She had finally mustered the courage to report the offence to the prime minister, who was forced to act and, because the staffer was a member of the government, had tried to diminish the seriousness of the offence and keep it under wraps for several days.

There was a huge outcry. A woman had been assaulted in government chambers by a fellow staffer. The prime minister had tried to sweep it under the carpet. And it was one more instance of female abuse, this time under the seal of political privilege.

The opposition launched a frenzy of accusations, calling for resignations, and predicting, more in hope than certainty, that it would topple the government. A protest march calling for government action against male abuse of women had already been organised. There were renewed calls for a Royal Commission.

Owen shifted uncomfortably in his chair. Daphne had started his day on a sour note, leaving him depressed, and now this. Reason told him these incidents were hardly similar to his own predicament, but they still fed his doubt. Had he been culpable? Was he answerable, and to whom? His thoughts wandered. The news had moved on to another story of woe, but he wasn't listening. His mind was elsewhere.

Suddenly the sound from the television went dead. Kate had entered without him noticing, and turned it off.

She had moved behind him, both arms around his neck. 'Come and talk to me, darling, while I make your favourite pumpkin scones.'

4

'You'll remember we spoke about the importance to learning of engaging students in verbal interactions with others and with the teacher, and not just having the teacher do all the talking. What are some of the ways we can do this?'

'Brainstorming.'

'Good, Oliver. That's an obvious way, isn't it. A natural beginning to lessons to find out what the children know, and to generate ideas. Come on, keep them coming.'

'Peer teaching.'

'Discussion.'

'Peer and self-assessment.'

'Conferencing.'

'What does that involve, Harriet?'

'The teacher talking to individual children about what they've learned, a one-on-one talk.

'Right. It's what I did then, asking Harriet to use language to explain a concept…to show what she's learned. Of course, because it's so intensive, teachers can probably only conference the same student once every fortnight. So we need to do more to promote thinking aloud. What is the most basic way of getting students to talk that we haven't mentioned yet?

'Questioning.'

'Good, Michelle. The staple diet of teaching is usually regarded as explanation and questioning.'

The lesson continued with Owen outlining the different types of questions, explaining their uses and giving examples.

As the class filed out, Michelle stayed behind as Owen was gathering his resources. 'Mr Barlow,' the normally extroverted Michelle was unsure of herself, 'you didn't seem to be yourself today.' She lowered her eyes, thinking she might have gone too far. It wasn't a student's business to be prying into a teacher's personal life.

'Why do you say that, Michelle?' Owen answered pleasantly. He knew he wasn't his usual sprightly self, but hoped that it hadn't shown.

Michelle was embarrassed, and was unsure what to say. It was more something she'd sensed. 'Sorry…I shouldn't have asked. Sorry,' and she turned to hurry from the room.

'Michelle,' Owen called her back. 'It was very kind of you to ask. I appreciate it. And you're right. I have a lot on my mind at the moment.'

Michelle's relief gave her encouragement. 'We all care about you, Owen.' She'd considered using the singular 'I care' rather than the royal plural, but decided against it. She patted his arm for a few seconds, and withdrew her hand hurriedly. 'I'll be late for Chemistry,' and she left the room quickly.

*

It was the day that had been set aside for his apology. The dean had organised the meeting with Natalie by email. Michelle had sensed a difference in Owen's mood, and her approach and concern for him after the tutorial made him feel better, but as the minutes crept by towards the meeting time, it proved to be a two-edged sword.

He was warmed by Michelle's concern, so much so that he felt the need to reach out to her, like she had to him, and that made him realise that it was the same impulse that led to his predicament with Natalie.

Michelle had patted his arm out of concern, and doubtless some affection for him. It would have been so natural to return the same, but he dared not. What might the repercussions have been? He felt safe with Michelle. But he had with Natalie too.

He understood the wisdom of rules forbidding physical contact with students, even when such minimal contact was natural and harmless, and while he had reached out to the mature-age Natalie, he knew it couldn't be left to the discretion of teachers. He'd heard too many stories of male teachers being too free and easy with students.

He'd thought about the apology for some time with a mixture of feelings. A bald 'I'm sorry' and a sudden retreat would not be sufficient, for her or for him. He needed to explain. He needed her to see the reason, to understand that his action was the result of caring. And he had to dispel the idea that he was a predator who took advantage of the vulnerable. If only she knew he'd been a great apologist for women confronting abuse.

The dean had arranged the meeting, telling Natalie she'd spoken to Mr Barlow, and he needed to speak with her to resolve the matter. So Natalie didn't know what to expect. The word 'apology' hadn't been mentioned to her.

Owen arrived first and sat uncomfortably in the small interviewing room. The carpet was deep green and slightly worn, there was a desk for more formal interviews and two facing lounge chairs in studded brown leather. Appropriate for affairs of state, if not affairs of the heart. He could hear laughter from a class down the corridor, but thankful that they would have privacy.

Natalie waited outside the room as though considering whether she should enter, before she knocked softly, and opened the door cautiously. She was dressed more formally than the usual student garb of torn and faded jeans and T-shirt. A tasteful navy blouse and beige skirt instead. She even wore a little make-up. Half-heels. Owen hardly recognised her, and regarded it as a statement. The formality of apology, or discussion of a complaint, demanded propriety.

She entered self-consciously, sat opposite him on one of the leather arm chairs, perching on the edge, rather than leaning back, knees together, ladylike, expectant. She hadn't made eye contact, and there was an awkward silence.

'I thought we had a real rapport, Natalie,' he began when Natalie didn't. He'd decided against beginning with the customary 'How are you?' 'We were so comfortable with each other.' He wanted her to look at him. She didn't, and it became apparent to Owen that this was as much a trial for her as it was for him. He was spared the gloating accuser.

She seemed to give a half nod, but looked uncomfortable, and sat with both hands clenched in her lap. It didn't seem to be the behaviour of the indignant victim demanding justice.

'You told me all about your marriage. Really personal things like your husband's affairs,' Owen said gently. He baulked at saying 'you remember'. That sounded too much like interrogation. He wanted to establish why he had reached out to her the way he had, a preamble to confessing to his overreaching. He tried to massage the thaw by recounting the personal nature of their conversation, and even revealing a similar experience in his own life. It didn't seem to make an impression. Better to be more direct.

'I kissed you because I felt moved by your situation. It was because I cared, Natalie. And you might remember leaning forward at the last moment so the kiss…well, it wasn't meant for your lips.'

She seemed to nod in agreement, and Owen thought he might be making headway. 'After what you told me about your marriage, I felt really sorry for you.'

He sensed her tighten, and realised the talk of his sympathy for her was a mistake. To be pitied was anathema. To act the way he had out of pity was probably worse.

'I'm not a sleaze, Natalie,' he whispered, feeling the heat at once behind his eyes. 'I detest men like that. Anyway, I'm sorry, really sorry, if I upset you. At the time, it felt like a natural thing to do, but it may have been foolish.'

Natalie cocked her head at the may have been, but quickly recovered, resuming her blank stare.

There was an awkward silence before he asked her if she had anything to say. It was a long time before she spoke. He waited patiently.

'I accept your apology,' she said in a whisper, a little huskily, and not looking at him. 'Thank you.'

She stood and turned to leave, uncertain of the departing courtesies for such an occasion. For a moment, turned towards him, she hesitated, about to speak, but the words didn't come, and she turned and hurried away self-consciously.

A few first-year students saw a well-dressed student dashing down the corridor past the tutorial rooms, the tears coursing down her face as she sought haven in the Ladies.

Owen sat quietly. It was uncertain for how long. He was relieved and disappointed. It was over and done with. Apology accepted. That was a relief. Still, he'd hoped for some shared analysis of the dynamics, and for her to have a deeper appreciation of why he'd acted as he did.

She might have shed some light on the impact it had on her, and why she saw fit to make a formal complaint rather than come to him. Was he that much of an ogre? But she didn't want to talk. He knew there was more involved for her.

He went to the staff common room to find several lecturers conferring loudly about their early classes. Owen thought they seemed more raucous than usual. He found their good cheer a challenge, and slipped away without being noticed.

*

'Put it behind you, Owen,' Kate tells him, having heard his account of the conversation. 'It's all over now. I'm proud of you.'

'Why?' Owen is surprised. He had no choice. He had to do it.

'You handled it well. You apologised when you really didn't do anything wrong. What happened between the two of you wasn't deserving of an apology. You could have argued about it with Lynne, and refused to do it.'

'No, I couldn't. She was only following official procedure.'

'Well, you've done it. It showed great humility. Who said the hardest thing for rational man to do is to apologise?'

'I think it was Thomas Hardy.' Owen was still downhearted. 'In one sense, it's all over. It won't go any further, I know that, but it's not over for me.'

Kate sat next to him putting an arm around his shoulders. 'It will go away, if you let it,' she said.

'If Natalie had at least said she was sorry too, regretted that it had been blown out of all proportion, or even admitted that I was only trying to be a comfort to her. She was so cold.'

'From what you told me, she might have been scared. At the very least, she mightn't have had any idea of how to behave. She might have had some power as the accuser, but she might have been feeling guilty about the fuss she'd made, and it was still a teacher-student power relation.'

'I thought I tried to make it as natural and warm as I could.'

'Owen,' Kate faced him, kneeling on the floor, in front of him, 'you're a great teacher, you take the job very seriously, but what's more important, you're a very sensitive and very caring person who tries to meet the needs of every student you teach. Never doubt it. This whole thing has been an unfortunate accident, a misunderstanding.'

'Thanks, Kate,' Owen answered, still not entirely convinced.

'No long face for Cassie!' she said cheerfully. 'She'll be home any minute.'

5

Owen stayed back at school for an awards night for the students when Blair came knocking at home. He asked Kate if he could see Owen, and at first was disbelieving when Kate told him Owen wasn't there. He even looked over her shoulder and down the hallway. It had only been two days since Lynne had spoken to Owen, so Kate didn't have to be told who the visitor was.

He was quite obviously hostile, and Kate decided it would be better to reason with him rather than send him on his way. That would only make him angrier, and more likely to cause trouble. She also reasoned it would be better for him to talk to her than to Owen. He wouldn't dare become violent with her.

She had a good idea what the visit was about, and ushered him into the study, so that Cassie, who was doing her homework upstairs, wouldn't be able to hear their conversation. That would really be upsetting for Owen.

'I believe your husband has been sexually abusing my wife,' Blair began, once he'd introduced himself. 'Of course, you'd know nothing about that,' he sneered.

Kate knew that hostility often fed hostility until the escalation was out of control, and was determined to stay calm. 'Well, you'd be wrong, Blair,' she said. The personal touch of using his name never hurt. 'My husband and I have discussed the matter in detail.'

Blair was thrown by this. He was always of the opinion that sexual abusers were always ashamed to speak of their exploits, particularly to wives or girlfriends. 'What did he say happened?' he asked aggressively, but not with as much hostility as before. 'I'd like to hear his version.' Perhaps it wasn't so bad if the wife knew about it.

Kate experienced a moment of indecision. She didn't know what Natalie might have told him. She might merely have hinted that something happened with Owen, or she might have blown it out of all proportion by suggesting he'd taken advantage of her. Kate could be forthright and admit to Owen's kiss, or she could try to discover what Blair had been told. She decided on the latter.

'What do you think happened, Blair? You're making the accusations,' she said calmly, hoping he'd take the bait. 'What did your wife tell you?'

'That they kissed!' Blair's hostility returned.

'Let me explain, Blair.' Kate knew now what she had to defend. 'Your wife was very upset and was telling Owen why she was so unhappy. I think Owen said she was crying. He tried to comfort her and, yes, he gave her a kiss, a little peck to show that he cared. It was nothing more than that. Nothing passionate. A small gesture of tenderness.'

'It was a kiss, and he's a teacher.'

'Yes, he is, and you could argue that he shouldn't have, but it was caring. It was hardly sexual abuse.' She wasn't going to reveal that Natalie didn't seem to mind at the time. That would cause big trouble. 'Men shake hands when they meet. Men and women exchange a kiss. Can I ask you, Blair, what your wife said about it?'

'They kissed.' He was a man of few words.

'But she didn't say my husband gave her a passionate kiss, or tried to…well, to take advantage of her, did she?'

Blair remained silent, and Kate knew the gamble of confronting him had worked. But the battle wasn't over. She knew that an irate Blair could still make trouble beyond the school.

'Blair,' she began gently, 'I want you to know that my husband is not only a fine teacher, but someone who cares very deeply for his students. He cared for Natalie. He could see she was hurting and he wanted to comfort her.'

Blair's mood changed dramatically. He slumped in his chair. The aggression had evaporated. Kate hadn't planned her last remarks beyond her need to defend Owen, but she realised that talking of Natalie's pain had made Blair feel vulnerable. She sensed the dynamic. Conflict between husband and wife. Husband culpable. An argument. The wife trying to make husband jealous.

'Did my wife tell your husband why she was so unhappy?' he asked tentatively. He wanted to know now what he might have been accused of doing.

This was another dilemma for Kate. Blair might be furious to find out that his wife had been airing their dirty washing to a teacher, or to anyone for that matter. Her good work so far might be under threat. She had to tread carefully, so she chose the middle ground.

'She said studying and running a house was proving difficult.'

That seemed to please Blair. It was no threat to him. It was even an admission of sorts that she was not doing the right thing by him. Kate was not going to mention the reports of Blair's affairs, and he seemed to be satisfied that Natalie hadn't.

'Kate, it is Kate, isn't it?' She had moved from enemy to confidante. He wanted to earn her approval. 'It really is hard, for me, I mean. She's not doing anywhere near what she used to do. I'm worn out when I get home, and sometimes…let's just say, things aren't what they used to be.'

'She's probably worn out too, Blair.' Kate thought of him sitting at the table demanding his dinner.

But Blair didn't seem to hear. 'And she wants to talk about what she's learned at uni. I sometimes feel she's trying to show me up. Things I've never heard before. Anyway, I just want to sit and relax in front of the TV.'

Kate had started to really dislike Blair. It was all right for him that Natalie was now carrying the burden of her studies. There was so much she was tempted to say. For instance, was he jealous that she was bettering herself? Wasn't he interested in what she learned or what her days were like? Didn't he want to share her dreams? Perhaps he might be a little less self-righteous if she confronted him with his affairs. But the fall-out would be terrible.

'Let me give you a woman's perspective, Blair,' she said, battling to hide her hostility. 'Natalie may want to become a teacher, not just because she'd enjoy it, or be good at it, but because she thinks you'd be really proud of her.'

'You reckon?' Blair wasn't convinced, but he did remember Natalie saying much the same thing.

'I don't know Natalie,' Kate began, 'but I think it's more than likely. And if she's happy doing what she wants to do, everything would be happier at home…for you both. Can I suggest something, Blair?'

'Sure.'

'I don't know if she has any late classes, but find out, and get the dinner ready, even if it's only once or twice a week. And even if it's heating up a takeaway. I know you're tired when you get home, but so is she. It'd make a big difference.'

'Thanks for the advice, Kate,' he said, getting up to leave. Advice he had no intention of heeding.

Kate watched as his utility did a dangerous U-turn and sped away. She should have felt well satisfied. The apology had been accomplished without a fuss, and any problems with Blair taking further action had been averted. But it had saddened her. She didn't know Natalie, but from what she knew of Blair, she knew that Natalie had a hard road ahead. It wasn't going to end well.

*

Owen began to catch a later bus in the mornings, and came home earlier when classes and meetings didn't demand his presence. His teaching was still sound but lacked his reputed energy and humour. The students noticed his lack of animation, and chatted about it among themselves. On a couple of occasions, Michelle mouthed 'OK?' when he looked in her direction, and he nodded back.

He abandoned working on the submission for a research grant for which he had recruited a team of colleagues. He did make sure another colleague was willing to lead the team.

He was pleasant at work but less gregarious, and seemed to spend more time closeted in his office, and away from the staff common room. He even stopped paying his two dollars for the weekly football tipping competition.

'You haven't been the same since, well, since our last talk a fortnight ago,' the dean, drawing him aside in the staff common room, commented. 'Is everything all right?'

'Yes, no problems,' Owen answered forcing a weak smile.

'It's not!' the dean said not unpleasantly. She of course understood why. Owen was a respected and popular member of the faculty, and she felt she knew him well enough to contradict, even to challenge. 'It's not anything to do with that unfortunate incident with the student, is it?' she asked, knowing that it was. She didn't wait for an answer. 'That's long forgotten. It was the tiniest indiscretion. I don't think you could even classify it as that. I'm quite sure she didn't blab about it, and none of the staff know. They'd never condemn you for it if they did know.'

'I've been thinking about retirement,' Owen replied, skirting the dean's question.

'But why?' the dean asked, shocked. 'Do you mean retirement or resignation from teaching? You're too young to stop working altogether. What would you do?'

Owen shrugged. He had thought about retirement, but hadn't considered what else he could do. Teaching was all he knew.

The dean was caught off guard, and concerned, both for Owen and the faculty. 'We need to talk about this further, Owen,' she said. 'Don't be too hasty. How does next Thursday suit at two thirty p.m.?'

Owen's lack of *joie de vivre* was even more apparent at home. He still asked Kate about her day, but seemed to be less engaged in listening. His usual ribbing of Cassie at the dinner table was replaced with polite enquiries.

One afternoon, Cassie returned home from school, barely able to contain her delight, having won a prestigious award for citizenship sponsored by the local Rotary Club. The award had been presented at a full school assembly by the local government member, and the Rotary Club leader asked her if she would speak at one of their meetings.

Owen was pleased, but embraced her tentatively, withdrawing quickly. He'd normally be excited and take pride in ringing the relatives, ask her twenty questions, but he asked none. She was hurt, and asked Kate if Dad was angry with her. They'd always been so demonstrative.

He abandoned some of the evening television shows he watched with Kate and Cassie, reality shows he lampooned as they shushed him, an after-dinner routine they all enjoyed, observed for the sake of family togetherness. Instead, he retreated to his study.

Kate was careful to choose the right moment to once again ask the inevitable question.

'I don't know what it is,' he told her that night as they undressed for bed, feeling miserable.

She felt that was barely a half-truth, yet she understood. She knew that sometimes the emotional impact of something trivial, a word or action, spreads through a person's being like a cancer. That a specific wound can result in a general pain.

'I did kiss her. Technically that's assault. Assault,' he repeated the word slowly, mulling over its implications. 'Sexual assault. I didn't mean any harm by it,' he said miserably.

Kate knew when to listen, and when to interject. They sat together on the edge of the bed. This was a time to listen.

'As I get older, more things become problematic. The clear-cut things we argued so passionately for in our youth don't seem to be so clear-cut any more.' Despite his sombre mood, he suddenly thought of Daphne Luscombe and her bigotry. He had to smile, but it didn't disprove his point. There were few certainties, and the most passionate arguments were sometimes a disguise for serious doubts.

Kate looked at him curiously, and waited. 'What isn't clear-cut?' she eventually asked. 'Are you referring to the business with that girl?' Kate hadn't told him of her meeting with Blair. That would have added fuel to the slow-burning fire.

'I wonder,' he replied, his thoughts racing ahead, 'if, when we get older, emotion and thought become even more…' he struggled for a word, 'cloudy. Do the boundaries lose definition, do the feelings become more diffuse, do the blacks and whites become grey…do they merge?'

'I'm not sure I understand the significance of merging emotion,' Kate queried after another long silence. 'What emotions do you mean?'

'I'm sure we shed our inhibitions, but do we also lose our moral compass?' Owen answered, patting her thigh and taking her hand. 'I wonder,' he repeated, and left the sentence unfinished, absorbed in his thoughts.

As they both sat together silently on the side of the bed, facing the window, Kate put her arm around his shoulders, tousling his hair. She liked to mother him. The stars outside bathed the sky in a feast of milky light.

A car turned into the gravel driveway next door. The engine stopped, a door slammed, and voices retreated to silence. Cassie could be heard laughing at something on the television downstairs.

'My poor silly boy,' Kate said, drawing the curtains to join him in bed.

6

'Dad, can you tell me what makes you tick?' Cassie's question was vague because she wanted a light-hearted opening, and not one that was confronting. If he had to ask the questions, it would save her from being too direct.

'Can you be a little more precise?' Owen replied with a smile.

'I want to know how men and women see relationships differently,' Cassie asked more seriously.

'Men and women, or boys and girls?' Owen could see what Cassie wanted to talk about. Damian. 'Are we talking about…about…'

'Yes, Dad. Relationships and sex too. And don't worry, I know all about the birds and the bees. I want your take on whether men and women are different in that way.'

Owen might have been a little embarrassed at first, but he was pleased she'd come to him. Talks of this sort had always been shared between mother and daughter, and sometimes behind closed doors.

Knowing that Kate was probably more qualified than him to discuss these matters, he realised what Cassie was doing. It was her way of reaching out to him. She knew he wasn't in a good place, though she didn't know why, and she wanted to make him feel valued, to feel that he was indispensable, at least to her. That was impressive maturity for a fifteen-year-old. He was overwhelmed with love for her.

'I think, Cassie,' he said, with a lump in his throat, 'you want to know how you might see relationships and sex differently from Damian.'

She nodded.

They were sitting together on the family room lounge bathed in the orange glow of a side table light, and she had linked her arm through his.

'When boys get to your age,' he began, feeling more confident, 'they probably think more about sex than girls, and feel more desire…and that's why Damian…'

'Yes, and apologised.' Cassie seemed pleased that Owen believed it to be a general truth, and not just Damian's weakness.

'Boys are thought to have more fantasies about sex than girls. Girls have fantasies too, but they are tied to committed relationships. Boy's fantasies are more…more physical. Am I making sense?'

'A lot of sense,' Cassie answered and leant against him. 'So Damian's like all other boys?'

'He feels the same tug of sexual desire as other boys, Cassie. But boys, and men, we're no different, have to show consideration for our partners, and listen to their needs.' Owen felt the need to put things in perspective.

There was a brief silence and Owen wondered what else he could contribute, but decided it was up to Cassie if she wanted him to say more. What detail did she want? He could hardly pry into the intimate aspects of her relationship with Damian, though he had no doubt it was innocent enough.

'It's been a big help, Dad,' Cassie added, and she meant it.

'What's been a big help?' Kate was standing in the doorway, a broad grin on her face, pleased father and daughter were having a deep and meaningful.

'Dad was telling me the facts of life.' Cassie smiled at Kate.

'Was he now?' Kate laughed. 'I didn't think he knew them.'

*

The following day was his meeting with the dean, and he caught the eight seventeen bus again, hoping to get to work early to order his thoughts. He'd made no firm decisions about what to say. His talk with Cassie had improved his spirits, but the uncomfortable feeling hadn't gone away. Talking of male sexual desire had kept the issue alive.

He knew the talk was Cassie's idea. If she'd consulted Kate, she would certainly have been discouraged from pursuing such a topic. Kate was well aware of his sensitivity.

He was surprised by the reaction of the bus passengers.

'Welcome back, stranger,' a voice called as he entered. Probably one of the university students.

'Good to see you,' Frank said benignly, holding his Tupperware container of biscuits on his lap with both hands. 'We've missed your moderating voice, Owen, to keep us all in check.'

Owen thought that very generous of Frank, who was surely the most moderate of the passengers.

Elizabeth made room for him next to her by moving her bag of office shoes, and placed a hand on his shoulder as he sat. He was startled by it, then pleased. What could be more natural, and welcoming?

There was even grudging acceptance from Daphne. 'You've been missed,' she said, but didn't say why, quickly burying her head in her latest Mills & Boon.

He felt buoyed by the trip. Simple friendship. People liked him. Whatever happened, he was no pariah.

*

He sat in his office watching the swaying gum trees drop pale-bellied leaves in the autumn blue, aware of the paradox that everything remains the same but won't stand still. He felt strangely removed from the rows of journals and shelved books, books that had engaged him lovingly over the years. A stack of assignments sat on his desk, ready for marking.

In half an hour, he would meet the dean. What would he say? He would be asked about retirement, probably cautioned against it. He would be told he still had a significant contribution to make, and that he was one of the most popular lecturers. She might tempt him with promotion. In a month or two, positions for senior lecturer and associate professor would be advertised. He knew he would have her endorsement. She obviously knew what bothered him. Or a small part of it anyway. She would try to reassure him, convince him that these misunderstandings were weekly fare in every large organisation, encourage him to confront his demons.

A rational part of him warned against being foolish, and leaving what he'd worked so hard to achieve, that the world was larger than his minuscule part of it, that life had limitless riches to offer, enough to pale his indiscretion, if it even was that, into insignificance.

He thought of Kate's playful kiss when he first told her what had happened with Natalie, Elizabeth's affectionate squeeze of his shoulder on the bus, Michelle's transparent concern in an empty classroom, and Cassie's loving ploy to stroke his ego.

He stood at the window. The gums were momentarily still. A group of students sat chatting on the lawn in a small circle with take-away coffees. An occasional tinkle of muted laughter was carried by a fickle breeze.

There was a light tap on the door, so gentle he assumed it was for a nearby office. A second tap, just as gentle, followed nearly half a minute later. He turned from the window to face the door, calling, 'Come in.' It had to be a student. A member of staff would knock and open the door without being invited.

Natalie, nervous yet purposeful, entered and moved quickly across to him by the window. Her eyes were lowered. She was in her usual student garb of jeans and pink cotton blouse. Owen was so surprised, he didn't react, didn't speak.

She stopped, leant forward, and rising on her toes, kissed him on the side of his mouth, half-opened in surprise. She turned wordlessly and left, without looking back, hurrying to the door and closing it softly behind her, but not before a flushed neck betrayed any attempted composure.

Owen moved to his desk and sat, deep in thought for several minutes. The gum trees whispered outside, the breeze caressing their branches. The sky was a rich blue. He felt suddenly liberated, a feeling of immense relief as if a giant hand had lifted a burden from him. I know what I'll tell the dean, he said to himself.